"You are…something else." Sasha smiled and shook her head, finding herself more engaged than she wanted to be.

She raised her glass to alert Jake that she needed another Brown Russian. Before long she'd polished off three. Suddenly Vince's jokes became outrageously funny, and Sasha laughed long and hard—and loud. Vince pulled his chair around closer to Sasha, until she could feel his breath on her neck. His cologne crept its way into her nostrils.

"You smell wonderful," she whispered.

His lips pressed themselves against hers, and his tongue teased the inside of her mouth. Whatever good sense she had was out the window as Vince took her to a new level of delight. His huge hand palmed her head and pulled her closer, and she wondered what that hand would feel like on her breast and even between her thighs. It had been a very long time since she'd even been kissed by a man. With his gentle touch, Vince had awakened every sensation in her, and she got lost in the moment. She simply got lost.

Books by Monica McKayhan

Harlequin Kimani Romance

Tropical Fantasy

MONICA MCKAYHAN

writes adult and young adult fiction. She currently has nine titles in print. Three are adult novels, and six are a part of an ongoing young adult series, Indigo Summer, and one young adult title, *Ambitious*. *Indigo Summer* was the launch title for Harlequin Kimani's young adult imprint, Kimani TRU, which made its debut in January of 2007. That same year in May, *Indigo Summer* snagged the #7 position on the Essence bestsellers list, another first for Kimani Press. It also appeared on the bestsellers list of *Black Issues Book Review* (BIBR), and was on the American Library Association's list of Quick Picks for Reluctant Young Adult Readers for three consecutive years.

She is a Certified Toastmaster (CTM) with Toastmasters International, and is also a member of the Black Women's Film Society. She lives in the Dallas area with her family.

To schedule an appearance, book a signing or interview with Monica, please email publicity@monicamckayhan.com.

TROPICAL
Fantasy

MONICA McKAYHAN

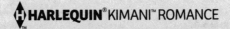
HARLEQUIN® KIMANI™ ROMANCE

Recycling programs
for this product may
not exist in your area.

ISBN-13: 978-0-373-86307-5

TROPICAL FANTASY

Copyright © 2013 by Monica McKayhan

H HARLEQUIN®
™ www.Harlequin.com

Printed in U.S.A.

Dear Reader,

Thank you for picking up *Tropical Fantasy*. As always, I appreciate your support.

Hopefully you will live vicariously through the lives of Sasha and Vince as they discover one another in the beautiful Bahamas. Sasha's a workaholic and is tough as nails, no doubt, but underneath that exterior she's vulnerable, as many of us are. She's convinced that she doesn't need a man—she simply needs her career. Making partner is the one thing that matters in her world, and there's no room for anything else. Vince is the perfect hero—the man's man. His charm will make your stomach tingle and your toes curl. And when you read the love scenes, you'll wish you were on Paradise Island with the two of them. Neither of them is perfect, yet by the story's end, they find that they're perfect for each other.

I hope that *Tropical Fantasy* will take you to places that you've never been before. It certainly took me to new heights in my writing process. My characters are always flawed, because people in general are flawed: there are no perfect people. That was the easy part. And I've always written about love. But the challenge in writing romance (for me) was taking sensuality to new levels—building characters that are comfortable in their sexual skin. If you've read any of my other books, you know that I've always held back, given just a little bit to be desired. Oh, but not this time. *Tropical Fantasy* will have you on the edge of your seats with every kiss, every whisper, every lovemaking scene.

I would love to hear from you! Visit my website at www.monicamckayhan.com and reach out to me. I also have a Facebook page and a MySpace page, and you can follow me on Twitter. Let me know what's on your mind.

My best to you always,

Monica McKayhan

God is the source of my talent and blessings.

My husband, Mark, makes sure that I have a comfortable environment in which to create my stories. My family is my backbone and motivation. Without the support from you guys, I wouldn't be able to do this. I love you!

This is for you, Granny. I miss you, but I'm glad that you left me so many little pieces of you. My life is so rich because you were here.

Chapter 1

Sasha glanced at the chipped nail on her right index finger. As much as she hated to admit it, she was in desperate need of a manicure. And she didn't even want to think about the ingrown toenail on her left foot. She also needed a pedicure something terribly. Arriving in time for the spa day with the rest of the bridal party wouldn't be all bad. In fact, it would be a welcome treat considering she hadn't visited her manicurist in the shop around the corner from her East Marietta subdivision in quite some time.

As she leaned back against the seat, she responded to a few emails from her iPhone and then sent her assistant, Keira, a text message asking her to reschedule her afternoon appointments. She sighed as she took a sip of her half-caf Americano and allowed her body to sink farther into the seat. She was exhausted, having spent most of the night packing—she'd sipped a cup of international coffee and stuffed clothing into her luggage well into the wee hours of the morning. Before long she'd fallen asleep fully clothed. Thankfully, she'd remembered to set her alarm clock.

She'd rushed to take a hot shower, and just as she'd put the finishing touches on her makeup, her doorbell rang. Peeking through the blinds, she spotted the charcoal-gray Lincoln Town Car parked in front of her house—the driver, a middle-aged black man dressed in a black suit, stood on her doorstep. Embarrassingly, she'd fallen asleep right there on the backseat of the car and didn't wake up until the Lincoln pulled up in front of Hartsfield-Jackson International Airport.

"We will now begin preboarding for Flight Number 1487 to Nassau, Bahamas…" The loud female voice shook Sasha back to reality.

After slipping her iPhone into a small compartment on the outside of her purse, she stood with her boarding pass in hand—it wouldn't be long after preboarding that first-class passengers would begin their ingression. She was anxious to get on the plane, because she knew that sleep would find her before the captain turned on the Fasten Your Seat Belts sign, and long before the flight attendants asked what she wanted to drink. She'd sleep through the entire flight and be refreshed when her little sister met her at the gate.

Her little sister was getting married, she thought and smiled. Little Bridget, who once wore French braids with colorful beads on the ends. She was the tender-hearted one who always cried during the hair-combing process—she always made such an unnecessary scene. Their mother would be so frustrated after dealing with Bridget that Sasha would end up with four cornrows down the center of her head instead of the French-braided love knot that she wanted so badly.

Bridget was definitely the baby of the family. She had their parents wrapped around her skinny little finger. Even now, as she insisted on a big wedding in the Bahamas instead of a quiet little ceremony at their family's church in Fayetteville, she'd far exceeded the budget that their father had set aside for her. And Sasha wondered if there'd be anything left for her in the event that she decided to get married someday. Although it seemed like a ridiculous thought at the moment, she hadn't completely ruled it out. However, she'd created a little nest egg of her own, just in case.

Soon she was on the plane, and as expected, slept through the entire trip. Next thing she knew, she'd arrived at her destination.

Nassau, with its arresting views of palm trees and clear blue skies, was exactly as Sasha had remembered it. Her family had vacationed there a few times and stayed at the same resort where Bridget's nuptials were scheduled to take place in the next day or two. She quickly gathered her luggage and stepped outside to look for her sister, who'd promised to meet her at baggage claim. Bridget was always fashionably late for everything, and Sasha often teased that she wouldn't make it to her own funeral on time. She glanced at her watch once more before pulling her iPhone out of her purse to give her sister a call.

"Hello, Sasha," a deep voice was saying, and when Sasha looked up she was staring into the deepest pair of brown eyes she'd ever seen. "I'm Vince. Vince Sullivan."

"Oh, yeah, Derrick's friend," said Sasha.

"I was sent by the bride and groom to pick you up

and ensure your safe arrival to the resort." He grinned a beautiful set of white teeth. His dimples were like little chocolate valleys, and Sasha couldn't help but stare.

"You're late," she said.

Towering almost two feet over Sasha's small frame, Vince smiled apologetically. "I'm sorry. I was asked at the last minute to pick you up as a favor to the bride. She had to rush off somewhere in a hurry—something about shopping for women's undergarments."

"Great. She could've just told me to grab a cab." Sasha sighed. "You didn't have to come all this way."

"It's okay, really. It wasn't very far. This *is* an island," he chuckled.

Sasha didn't find a bit of humor in his comment, nor did she find it cute that her sister had sent her fiancé's best friend to *fetch* her from the airport. She tried with everything in her to be annoyed, but every time she caught a glance at those sexy brown eyes, she found herself mesmerized. He awakened things in her that she didn't even know were there, and it confused her. As an attorney, she took pride in being in control, but something about Vince made her anything but. His presence made her unsettled, a bit anxious. She couldn't understand it at all. What was wrong with her? She'd seen handsome men before. In fact, she'd met Vince before—on a couple of occasions.

Their first meeting had been a nightmare for Sasha. She'd backed into his car while trying to parallel park along the street in front of Derrick's condo. She'd been apologetic, yet he'd made her feel as though she'd committed a crime. He'd accused her of being too preoccupied, and she thought he was making too big of a fuss over a small ding.

"You can barely see the scratch," she'd said.

"This is a custom paint job," he'd claimed, "Do you know how much this is going to cost to repair?"

"I have insurance," Sasha spat. "I'm sure they'll take care of it."

And they had taken care of it, sending her premium through the roof. She'd developed a strong opinion of Vince in the process—he was arrogant.

Today he seemed much taller, and way more gorgeous. And had he always owned that deep set of dimples? She couldn't, for the life of her, remember seeing them before. She was being ridiculous! Simply experiencing jet lag. And for that, she had the perfect remedy—a nice, long afternoon nap once she made it to her hotel quarters.

"Is this your only bag?" Vince was asking as he grabbed the handle of her suitcase.

"Yes," she replied and suddenly wished she'd gone to the restroom and freshened up a bit, checked her hair. She hoped it wasn't all over her head or smashed down in the back from the snooze she'd taken earlier.

She followed Vince to the silver Mercedes that was parked curbside with the flashers on. He popped the trunk and placed her bag inside.

"Can I take your smaller bag too?" he asked, pointing at her carry-on Coach bag. She handed it to him and he placed it in the trunk also. He moved around to the passenger's side of the car, which happened to be the opposite side of cars in the United States. He held the door open for her until she slid onto the leather seat. She watched as he took his place behind the wheel of his rented vehicle.

"Doesn't it confuse you—driving on the opposite side of the car?"

"I love a challenge." He grinned that mesmerizing grin again.

"It seems silly, especially when most car rental places offer cars that are created the right way."

"The right way?"

"Yes, with the steering wheel on the proper side of the car."

"Proper according to whom?" Vince asked.

"According to car makers in the U.S. of A.," said Sasha.

"Last time I checked, we weren't in the U.S. of A." He maneuvered the car into traffic and spoke in his best Bahamian dialect. "Ve're in da islands of da Bahamas, with its clear blue skies, sandy beaches and da best conch fritters dis side of da hemisphere."

Sasha laughed—she couldn't help it. He sounded so ridiculous, yet he was cute in his own little way. And he had a sense of humor.

"Yeah, I wish I was on the other side of the hemisphere—in the U.S. of A. right now," she said.

"Instead of here…in the beautiful Bahamas?"

"Yes, this wedding couldn't have come at a worse time for me," Sasha complained.

"Really? Why?"

"My office is hosting its annual retreat this weekend in Savannah, and I'm missing it. My sister's nuptials are putting a real damper on my schedule," she mumbled.

"Wow, you must be a workaholic," said Vince.

"I'm not a workaholic. My career is just very important to me."

"It's your sister's wedding. Isn't that important too?" Vince glanced over at Sasha and pierced her with those brown eyes.

"Of course it's important. It's just…I just…well, it was just not a good time for me."

"Are you really that shallow?" Vince asked. "There's nothing more precious than family."

Had he just called her shallow?

"I beg your pardon. You don't know anything about me! And I'm not shallow."

"I'm sorry for calling you shallow. I meant to say that you made a shallow comment."

"I'm just saying…why couldn't she just do a simple little ceremony in Atlanta? Why fly to another country just to say 'I do'?"

"You should consider it an honor to stand up for your sister on such an important day."

"I have things going on in my life right now," Sasha retorted. "And this trip here, right now…this is inconvenient."

"That's too bad," said Vince. "You're completely missing it."

"Oh really?" Sasha asked. "So I guess you have it all figured out."

"I have a pretty good handle on things. I know what's important. In fact, when Derrick asked if I could fly to the Bahamas and be the best man at his wedding, I didn't give it a second thought. I knew I had to be here."

"How noble of you," Sasha said sarcastically and then stared out the window at the palm trees as they rushed past. She was done talking to this man.

An awkward silence suddenly resonated through the car, and Vince adjusted the volume on the stereo. As the sound of Caribbean rhythms filled the air, Sasha pulled her iPhone out of her purse and checked her email. The music wasn't very successful at drowning the silence, and the short drive seemed so much longer than it really was. Sasha wished her sister hadn't sent Vince to pick her up from the airport. She'd have been more comfortable taking a taxi. At least the driver would've kept his opinions to himself.

"I have to make a quick stop along the way," Vince said. "I hope you don't mind."

"You've got to be kidding."

"Not at all. Won't take but a sec."

Soon Vince pulled into Potter's Cay, the island's fish market and fruit stand tucked away under the Paradise Island Bridge. Potter's Cay, a place where Bahamians shopped for the fresh catch of the day and the freshest produce on the island, was an attraction that Sasha and her family had visited on occasion.

"What are we doing here?"

"I'm in the mood for fresh snapper."

"Fish?"

"There's nothing like it." Vince smiled as he turned off the engine and removed the keys from the ignition. "Let's go."

"Let's go?"

"It's pretty hot, and you'll roast in the car without air-conditioning." He smiled but still seemed adamant that she get out of the car.

She immediately caught the smell of conch fritters and fried fish. She and Vince strolled along the sidewalk, taking in the eclectic stalls where food vendors sold their freshly cooked items. Friendly female vendors sat placidly in front of fruit and produce stalls bursting with bananas, plantains, papaya, red peppers, tomatoes and yams. In front of many stalls were cages of swarming black crabs and other seafood. Fishermen in rubber boots hoisted giant bags of fresh fish and cleaned the catch of the day with sharp knives right there as customers looked on.

Interspersed among the row of stalls serving cooked food were several stands selling fresh fish. The constant calls of "fresh fish, fresh fish," were heeded by car after car of customers who pulled up next to the street-side stall for plastic bags filled with fresh snapper.

Vince stepped up to a fresh fish vendor and said, "I'd like a pound of snapper, please."

"Some fresh conch salad too, sir?"

"Yes!" he exclaimed and gave the brown Bahamian woman a warm smile. "I love it."

"What about you, my lady?" The woman smiled at Sasha. "Fresh conch salad or a conch fritter?"

"No, thank you."

"What? You have to have one or the other," said Vince.

"I don't…I don't eat that."

"I'll have conch salad," said Vince, "and one for the lady too."

"I said I didn't want any," Sasha said, but Vince wasn't listening.

The Bahamian woman handed each Vince and Sasha a bowl of the native fare. Sasha reluctantly took hers, wondering who Vince thought he was—ordering for her like that and insisting that she taste something she wasn't accustomed to eating. He was presumptuous and arrogant, she thought. But she tasted it, and it was delightful against her tongue. She'd never tried it before; the name *conch* just didn't appeal to her. She'd always wondered how something with such an ugly name could possibly taste good.

Not wanting Vince to know that she was enjoying her salad, she toyed with the fork a bit, picking over the food. They moved down the sidewalk to a fresh produce stand, where Vince purchased tomatoes, bell peppers and onions. He seemed to know his way around the island and carried himself as a native. If it weren't for the crisp slacks, polo shirt and shined shoes that he wore, he could've easily been mistaken for an islander. The precision haircut and carefully manicured nails were a dead giveaway also. She immediately admired his confidence, although she hated to admit it.

"So, obviously you cook," Sasha stated.

"I do," Vince said. "What about you?"

"I dabble a little. I always said that if I didn't make it as a lawyer, I'd become a chef."

"What's your specialty?" he asked.

"Deep-dish pizza," she boasted, "and I make my own crust."

"Really? That's impressive," he said. "Are you part Italian?"

"No," she answered with a laugh. "What's your specialty?"

"Fried chicken, fried fish, fried pork chops..."

"Don't you know that fried foods are bad for your health? That's why everyone in the black community suffers with high blood pressure."

"I know, but it's so darn good," he admitted. "My arteries are probably already clogged with fried fish grease."

"You should try baking your chicken, fish and pork chops," Sasha said. "It's much healthier."

"I'll consider that," he said. "Maybe you can show me how it's done."

Sasha realized that she'd let her guard down and needed to put her wall of resistance back up. She said, "I doubt it."

* * *

"Velcome to da Bahamas," said the chocolate-brown man as he swung her door open and held it for her while she climbed out of the car. He wore a red concierge uniform, with a name tag that read Robert. Robert's graying hair and beard seemed to be a little matted, but his eyes were a pair of the friendliest ones that Sasha had ever seen. "Right this way, please."

He escorted her through the massive lobby, with its buffed floors and modern furniture. Women in short skirts moved their hips to the sounds of Caribbean music being played by a live band. As the music filled the air, a young woman greeted her with a tray filled with beverages.

"Rum punch, my lady?" the woman asked in a soft voice.

Sasha checked her watch. It was nine-thirty in the morning, a bit early for something harder than orange juice.

"Sure. What the heck?" said Sasha as she grabbed a glass and headed for the counter to check in.

A group of women dressed in bikinis and giggling like teenagers headed in her direction.

"Sasha! You made it." Bridget was wearing a white bikini with a blue sarong draped across her hips. She gave Sasha a tight squeeze. "I'm so glad you're here. Your mother is really working my nerves—between her and Aunt Frances, I don't know who's worse. But you're here now. You can run some interference for me. Give them someone else to drive crazy."

"Hey, Sasha." Their cousin Vanessa popped up from among the crowd and hugged her. "Girl, we have to do something with this hair of yours." She brushed Sasha's bangs from her face.

"Our hair appointment is at eleven. Will you be checked in and ready to go in an hour?" Bridget asked.

"I'll do my best." Sasha managed a smile and then caught a glimpse of Vince.

He was engaged in a conversation with the concierge, and she couldn't help but stare. Her eyes traced his hairline and then made their way down to the curve of his strong cheekbone.

"Did you hear me, Sash?" Bridget was asking.

"No, I'm sorry. What did you say?"

"Was Vince the perfect gentleman? I warned him to be nice."

"Oh, yeah. He was just…fine," Sasha said, "but next time, I can get a cab. It wasn't necessary for him to come."

"He insisted," Bridget explained. "Besides, he rented that stupid car and thinks he knows his way around the island."

"He can pick me up anytime, anywhere with his fine self," said Deja, Bridget's friend since elementary school. Even with a full figure, she still managed to squeeze an oversized set of caramel-colored breasts into a yellow bikini top. "He doesn't even know how fine he is."

"Don't be so brazen, Deja," said Kim, Bridget's tall, slender friend wearing a one-piece bathing suit. She pulled her long sandy-colored hair into a ponytail. "Less is definitely more."

"Sasha, we'll meet you here in an hour. We're taking a water taxi to the salon," said Meka, Bridget's other maid of honor. She was carrying a notepad and following along on Bridget's heels.

"Fine, I'm gonna get a shower and relax for a minute. I'll see you all later." Sasha smiled and then took a long sip of rum punch.

Chapter 2

The view was breathtaking—a picturesque scene of turquoise waters and white sand. Sasha wanted nothing more than to slip into a sundress—one of six that she'd purchased at Macy's last summer—and relax on her patio for the rest of the morning. She opened the blinds in the living room of her condo to let the sunshine in, and then hit the power button on the stereo. She slipped her shoes from her aching feet and brushed her toes against the red carpet. The decor in the condo was beautiful—a mixture of tropical colors: red, blue, yellow and green. She danced her way into the bathroom and started the shower.

As the warm water began to cascade over her body, thoughts of Vince popped into her head. What was he doing there—in her head? Especially when she didn't particularly like him. He'd been rude and insulting. But no matter how hard she tried, she couldn't get his face out of her mind. He was sexy and had a great smile—the two things that she found most appealing about a man. The two things that were at the top of her list, just below intelligent, educated and successful. But he couldn't be all of those things without substance. He needed a heart and soul. He had to have character and love his mama. And he couldn't be boring. He needed a sense of humor, and he had to be romantic.

She knew it was a lot to ask, which is why she'd been single for so long. She wouldn't settle again. Not as she had with Kevin. He'd been sexy all right—taught her to explore her own body and to let go of her inhibitions. He was even intelligent and educated, but that's where it stopped. His soul was empty, and he had been selfish. He'd hung on to her coattail for years with talk of doing something with his degree in architecture, but never following through. She'd funded too many business ventures that had nothing to do with architecture, and all had failed to produce any substantial income. But she loved him, and for that reason she hadn't seen any of the red flags.

She stepped out of the shower and wrapped the thick robe around her body. The local radio station was playing a Rihanna tune and Sasha sang along. She pulled her laptop out of its bag and logged on, deciding to answer a few emails before meeting Bridget and the crew in the lobby. She decided to give Keira a call and see if she'd received any messages.

"You are on vacation, Miss Thing. Why are you calling me?" Keira asked, with attitude. "Do you know how expensive international calls are?"

"I'm just checking in," Sasha explained. "Anything going on?"

"Nothing I can't handle. You having a good time?"

"The weather is beautiful, and I love my condo," said Sasha.

"But?" Keira detected something in her voice.

"I need to be in Savannah for that retreat. I feel like Kirby's up to something."

Kirby. The Antichrist is how Sasha often described her. She came on board soon after Sasha had been promoted to senior associate. She had been an intern—fresh out of law school. Sasha had taken Kirby under her wing and taught her everything she knew. She immediately liked Kirby because she was energetic and ambitious, yet modest and conservative. She was like a sponge, absorbing everything, and Sasha loved her enthusiasm. She wasn't even surprised when Kirby was quickly promoted to junior associate. But soon after Sasha noticed a change in Kirby—her long conservative skirts soon became four inches shorter and her blouses became more tight-fitting and showed more cleavage than necessary. And she was spending way too much time with the firm's senior partner, Kyle Johnson. With the two of them behind closed doors, it was obvious that something more was going on than practicing law. And when Kirby became a senior partner in half the time it took Sasha to achieve such a feat, she knew she'd have to step up her game just to stay above water.

Sasha didn't have a problem with Kirby's accomplishments—even if she had pretty much slept her way to the top. But it was the sudden cockiness and the disrespect that Kirby displayed toward Sasha that she couldn't deal with. It was as if Kirby had forgotten where she'd come from and had made it her point to compete with Sasha on every little thing. She wanted the corner office with the view that Sasha had had her sights on since the day she'd walked into Johnson, John-

son and Donovan. With older partner Louis Johnson retiring soon, one of the two ladies would be promoted.

"Of course she's up to something. She wouldn't be
Kirby if she wasn't. But you'll be there soon enough. I
have you booked on a red-eye tomorrow night. You'll
be there first thing Saturday morning. You won't miss a
thing," said Keira. "If anything goes down before then,
you'll be the first to know."

"Okay."

"Now, please try and enjoy yourself. You're in the
Bahamas, for crying out loud! And it's your sister's
wedding. Try to be there for her, Sasha."

"I'll do my best," Sasha said, smiling at her assistant's advice.

Over the past two years, Keira had become more
than just an assistant. She'd become Sasha's friend—
someone she trusted and confided in. If anyone knew
Sasha well, it was Keira. Keira could see right through
Sasha's hard exterior. As soon as Sasha made partner,
her first business decision would be to give Keira the
raise she deserved. Being a single parent with three
children made it hard for Keira to make ends meet, but
Sasha intended to change all that.

"Now, get off my phone, Sasha Winters. You are not
allowed to call me anymore today. Unless you're calling
to tell me that you met some sexy Caribbean hottie on
the beach and he's about to ravish you without mercy."

"You've been reading too many romance novels,"
Sasha said with a laugh.

"It could happen," Keira said. "Now, if you don't
mind, I have a client on hold. Take lots of photos and
send me a few by text message."

"Will do."

"And Sasha—" Keira put on her serious voice "—try to have fun."

"I will."

She hung up, logged off of her computer and decided on a strapless white sundress.

With a few minutes to spare, Sasha decided to take a quick tour of the resort. She took in the gorgeous palm trees blowing in the wind just outside her door. The beautiful ocean with waves crashing against the shore caught her attention as she made her way to the front of the resort. The three pools and Jacuzzi mandated that she find time for some relaxation. She ended up at the poolside bar and climbed onto a wooden stool.

"I'll just have a ginger ale with a lemon wedge," she said to the bartender.

"And I'll have what she's having," said a familiar voice.

Vince climbed onto the bar stool next to hers. Immediately she felt a tingle in the pit of her stomach. His cologne was intoxicating.

"I was hoping to bump into you," he said.

"Me? Why?" she asked. "So that you could insult me some more?"

"I owe you an apology. I was a bit rude earlier today. Accusing you of being a workaholic," he said.

"And shallow," Sasha reminded him, "and insisting that I eat conch salad when I said I didn't want any."

"Yeah, that too." He smiled and raised his glass to her. "Truce?"

"Truce," she said, raising her glass to his.

"But you enjoyed the conch salad. I saw you secretly eating it and scraping the bowl."

"I wasn't scraping the bowl!"

"You all but licked your fingers," he teased.

"You're a trip."

"So I've been told," he said with a smile. "So…what are you getting done at the salon today? Your hair is already very beautiful." He unexpectedly brushed his fingertips against her forehead and pushed her bangs from her eyes.

Who gave him permission to touch her?

Once she gathered herself, she said, "I'll probably just have it shampooed and styled for the wedding. And I'm long overdue for a manicure." She reached her hand out to show him her fingernails.

He grabbed her hand in his in order to get a better view of her tattered nails, and it felt as if a surge of electricity rushed through her. Her bare nipples strained against the fabric of her sundress. They instantly became erect, and she hoped he hadn't noticed. There was no doubt this man's touch did things to her body. She was definitely attracted to him, no matter how much she tried to deceive herself. The feeling reminded her of the eighth grade when Todd Valentine had grabbed her hand and leaned in for a kiss. Her heart had pounded and her stomach had done somersaults. This was ridiculous— feeling this way about a man like some silly schoolgirl.

"Your nails aren't that bad," Vince said as he caressed every one of her fingers with his thumb. She wondered what she would do if he placed one of her fingers into his mouth.

"So you made it." The sound of her mother's voice killed whatever moment she was having with Vince. "I've been all over this property looking for you!"

"Mother. Hi." Sasha hopped from the barstool and gave her mother a hug. She peeked over her mother's shoulder and noticed her father standing there, too. "Hi, Daddy."

"Hello, sweetheart," her father said and went in for a kiss on the cheek. "Glad you made it in safely."

"You both know Vince, right? Derrick's friend. Um…he's the best man."

"Of course," Brian Winters reached his hand out to Vince for a firm handshake. "We're still on for this afternoon, right?"

"Of course, sir. Looking forward to it."

Sasha wondered what Vince and her father had planned for the afternoon.

"The girls are waiting for you in the lobby," Charlotte Winters said, casually changing the subject. "If you don't get going, you'll be late for your appointment."

She felt as if she should say something to Vince, like *hope to see you later*, but there was no time. Her mother nearly dragged her down the sidewalk toward the lobby.

Rubbing her fingertips across Sasha's brow, Charlotte said, "Sasha, make sure that you do something with these eyebrows. Get them arched. And make sure that when you get your manicure that your nail polish is a neutral color. Nothing outlandish. In fact, just a French manicure would do just fine."

"Ma, please."

"I know you're conservative, sweetie. You don't really need this speech, but some of these girls just don't know any better. Those girlfriends of Bridget's…" Charlotte lowered her voice to a whisper, "…one of them is actually wearing a tattoo, right there on her boobs. What is this world coming to?"

"Ma, she's young." Sasha knew that her mother was referring to Deja. "And it's trendy to have a tattoo there. I think it's cute."

"Cute? It seems slutty to me," said Charlotte. "How is that going to look in the wedding photos? The dresses are low-cut, and…"

"Ma, no one will even see it in the photos." She couldn't understand why she was even having a conversation about the boobs of Bridget's friend with her mother. She thought it more appropriate for her mother to have this conversation with the bride. Or even Deja for that matter, "Ma, I love you. We'll talk later…when I get back. I promise."

It wasn't unusual for Sasha to have conversations like this with her mother. In fact, they disagreed about most things. Even if Sasha had said the sky was blue, her mother would have challenged her and sworn that it was red. If Sasha had said up, Charlotte Winters would have strongly said down. When Sasha had settled on law school and decided to follow her father's career path, it was as if Charlotte's hopes and dreams for her daughter were lost. She'd wanted Sasha to do something more meaningful—such as being her first daughter to marry, becoming a homemaker, and giving her some grandchildren. Those were Sasha's duties as a daughter. Women didn't pursue such careers. They married men who pursued those careers.

Sasha had been unable to completely please her mother. It seemed that while she couldn't do anything right, Bridget was the one who favored her mother. She would be the first to marry, she'd be the perfect homemaker, and she'd give their mother beautiful grandchildren. Bridget had gone to college, but instead of pursuing a career in her field of accounting, she'd opened a little boutique—sold items on consignment, which barely took care of the overhead. But that was fine, because she'd managed to snag a great husband in the process. And she showed up for Sunday dinners.

After kissing her mother's cheek, she caught up with Bridget and the rest of the bridal party. They were already climbing into the back of a black SUV when Sasha took the front passenger's seat and secured her seat belt. The SUV made its way out of the resort's circular drive and down the hill. As they drove down Bay Street, Sasha noticed the straw market and made a mental note to stop there on the way back. She loved the shops and fraternizing with the Bahamian women who peddled their handmade souvenirs. She loved the Bahamas.

They took a water taxi to the spa on Paradise Island, where they were greeted with glasses of wine and fresh fruit. With an herbal-scented green mask on her face, Sasha relaxed while a young Bahamian woman rubbed her feet with hot oils and another manicured her nails. She closed her eyes and savored the moment. It had been months since she'd enjoyed a manicure and pedicure. Bridget sat in the leather chair next to hers.

"Thank you for coming, Sash. It really means the world to me that you're here," said Bridget.

"Glad I could be here for you," said Sasha.

"I know that it's not the most convenient time for you, but I appreciate the sacrifice that you made."

"Don't sweat it," said Sasha, closing her eyes again.

"I love you, Sasquatch," said Bridget, using her pet name for Sasha that had stuck through the years.

They'd been close once—inseparable even. That was long before Kevin had shattered Sasha's heart, and before she'd buried herself in her work to escape the pain. Her sister had been her best friend and confidante, but all that changed when Sasha decided to shut everyone out of her life and to make her career a priority. Nothing else mattered except passing the bar. And once she'd accomplished that, her journey from intern to junior associate was inevitable. It wasn't long before she'd snagged a senior associate position, and in just six years, she was already being considered for partner.

Sasha hadn't been on vacation in three years. There was never time. She barely made time for hair appointments, manicures or pedicures. More often than not, she'd stop by Ray's in the City—one of her favorite restaurants—for takeout on her way home. She'd grab a bottle of wine and eat dinner alone in her large kitchen, with its stainless steel appliances and hardwood floors, law books scattered about in front of her. She had a knack for cooking—was an undercover chef. Had law school not worked out, she'd have gone to culinary school, she often thought. She was a great cook. Yet, her evenings had been reduced to expensive takeout and a bottle of Chardonnay to wash it all down.

"I wish you wouldn't call me Sasquatch," Sasha told her sister. "I'm not a big, hairy Bigfoot-looking thing."

Sasha was far from big. With her petite frame, medium-brown complexion and short bob haircut, she often turned heads when she walked through downtown Atlanta wearing one of her tailored suits and her designer heels.

"I think it's a cute nickname," Bridget said with a giggle. "You're too uptight, Sasha. You need a man."

Sasha was tired of people telling her what she needed. Just a few hours earlier she'd had a confrontation with Vince, and then had to deal with her mother, who always told her she needed to spend more time with the family, needed to show up for more Sunday dinners. And now her sister was swearing that she needed a man, which, in her opinion, was the last thing that she needed. Men always complicated things, got in the way. What she needed was that corner office with the view of the city.

"Have you sworn off men forever, Sash?"

"No, not forever. Just for right now," said Sasha.

"You think you might get married someday?" Bridget asked, out of the blue. "Are you ever going to forget about what Kevin did and settle down with someone new?"

"I don't know, Bridge. I'm really married to my career right now. And I like it that way."

"Your career can't keep you warm at night, or take you on romantic walks through Piedmont Park," said Bridget. "And what about sex? When was the last time you…?"

"Bridget, please!" Sasha eyeballed the Bahamian woman who was massaging her feet and wondered if she was eavesdropping. The woman smiled as if she was waiting for Sasha's response to her sister's inappropriate question.

"I'm just asking. I mean, there are probably cobwebs in there. And everybody needs a little maintenance every now and then," Bridget told her.

"See, this is exactly why you and I don't have these types of conversations."

"I'm sorry, Sash. I'm just teasing." Bridget smiled, then said, "But seriously, don't you want to get married and have some babies one day?"

"One day…yes."

"I know you don't like to be set up, Sasha, but I was thinking…"

"Oh, here we go," Sasha groaned.

She knew that her sister was probably about to fix

her up with Vince, which is why she'd sent him to the airport instead of coming herself. She'd wanted the two of them to hit it off. And Sasha could understand why—Vince was gorgeous. As a matter of fact, he'd danced around in her thoughts since the moment she'd left the resort. But she didn't appreciate being set up, and she was tired of people thinking that it was okay. She was fine being single.

"Paul," said Bridget. "He's one of Derrick's grooms-men. He's the fair-skinned one. Not very tall, but he's such a sweetheart, Sash."

Such a sweetheart. Interpretation: "He's not very attractive."

"When I found out that he was a judge in DeKalb County, I knew the two of you would hit it off—seeing as though you're in the same line of work and all. I can't wait to introduce you to him. I told him all about you."

"What? No more matchmaking, Bridget."

"He graduated from Harvard…cum laude."

"That's nice," Sasha said sarcastically.

"And he's single," Bridget urged, "drives a Maserati. Can you believe that? How many black men you know are driving around the city of Atlanta in a Maserati?"

"Not very many."

Sasha was ready for the conversation about Paul to be over. She'd seen Paul once or twice and hadn't found him the least bit interesting. He was the type her mother would choose for her. No matter what he did for a living or what type of car he drove, he definitely wasn't her type. Although she hated to admit it, the truth was she was more interested in knowing more about Vince.

"So how long has Derrick known Vince?" Sasha asked, trying not to appear to be interested.

"Girl, all his life. They grew up together. Same high

school…same college," said Bridget, "but Paul he hasn't known very long. A couple of years maybe."

"He seems a little arrogant," Sasha said. "Vince, I mean."

"He comes off that way sometimes, but Vince is a nice guy. And he's good-looking too, but not really your type. You're career-minded. He's a dreamer."

"What do you mean *dreamer?*"

"He doesn't really take life seriously. I mean he has a degree in dentistry, for Christ's sake. He should have his own private practice or work in one of those upscale dental offices in Buckhead. Instead he chooses to work at that low-income health center in the heart of Atlanta for nothing, giving away his services for free. He's got a little matchbox office down there and he makes a small stipend, but I'm sure it's pennies compared to what he could make. Might as well go work at McDonald's."

"Isn't that noble? I mean, giving back to his community and all?"

"Noble? I think it's absurd."

"Our father did the same thing for years, Bridget. As a young attorney, he worked for Legal Aid, and he offered his legal services pro bono to many underprivileged people over the years."

"Thanks to Mama, he didn't completely lose his mind though. Thank God she talked him into working for that law firm and making a decent living for us. It's because of that firm that we were able to live the way we did."

"But Daddy wasn't happy at that firm. He was happier serving others."

"Serving others is fine, but it doesn't put food on the table, nor does it secure the future of your children. Which is why I'm marrying Derrick. Besides the fact that he's drop-dead gorgeous and can give me beautiful babies, he's successful and he's the sole heir to his father's business. My children will have the best of the best."

"So you're not marrying for love?"

"Of course I'm marrying for love! It's just that love wasn't exactly at the top of my list. It was just below 'Must have six-figure salary,'" said Bridget with a giggle. "But don't get me wrong, Sasha. Love is important. And I hope that you find it someday, or it finds you."

"Well, I'm not exactly looking," said Sasha.

"That's okay. Sometimes love finds you anyway. Especially when you're not looking," Bridget said. "Just make sure when it finds you it comes with a nice 401(k)."

"You're a mess!" Sasha exclaimed and laughed.

"I know, but you love me anyway."

"I do love you, sis, but your view of life is pretty twisted. Derrick had better make sure he has a prenup in place," teased Sasha. "Have him give me a call and I'll draw up the papers for him. There are still a few hours before the wedding."

"He's already had one drawn up," Bridget said candidly.

"Really?" Sasha asked, rising in her chair to give her sister a closer look. "How did you feel about that?"

"It's okay. I mean, he's not going anywhere and neither am I. Besides, our future is already secured."

"What's that supposed to mean?" Sasha asked.

Bridget laid a gentle hand on her stomach, and smiled.

"You're pregnant!" Sasha exclaimed.

"Shh. Keep it down," Bridget whispered. "I don't

want anyone knowing before it's time. Except you, Sasha. I can trust you."

"How far along?"

"About seven weeks."

"You haven't told Derrick yet?"

"He can't know before the wedding," said Bridget.

Sasha gave her sister a sideways look.

"Don't look at me like that, Sasha. It's complicated," Bridget whispered. "He's got this…this plan. It's so stupid. He says he doesn't want children until two years after we're married."

"Then why didn't you respect his wishes?"

"Who can live with that kind of pressure? Two years is a long time, and I'm not getting any younger. I hate clichés, but my biological clock is ticking. And I know that once this baby comes and he lays eyes on it, he'll change his mind."

"What if he doesn't?"

"He will."

"You're not trying to…you know…replace the other baby, are you?"

Bridget dropped her head, didn't want to respond.

"One doesn't have anything to do with the other."

"Doesn't it?"

"That was so long ago, Sasha. I was a kid. And I'd managed to forget all about it until now. Thank you very much."

Bridget's abortion wasn't something that could easily be forgotten. Sasha remembered how well her sister had hidden the pregnancy. But it wasn't long before Charlotte Winters caught wind of it. And when she did, there was no conversation about it—abortion was inevitable. Keeping it was never an option for Bridget. Their mother had worked too hard to build a perfect image for her daughters. A teen pregnancy would've tarnished that image beyond repair, and Charlotte Winters wasn't having that.

Sasha remembered the tragedy as if she'd had the abortion instead of Bridget. She remembered the dull gray walls at the abortion clinic, and the Hispanic lady who handed them a ton of papers to sign. She remembered the pain in her sister's eyes and the deep sadness on her face. She'd also remembered the grueling whimpers as Bridget cried herself to sleep that night. It was the saddest time in both their lives, and for that she blamed their mother. Their father would never have allowed such a thing to go on. They weren't allowed to breathe a word of it to their father, or anyone else, for that matter. Sasha thought it to be a horrible secret for young girls to be forced to keep, but she had no choice. They simply did as they were told. In fact, they never even talked about it again between themselves—until now.

Sasha recognized her sister's need to replace the unborn child she'd once lost, but she was going about it all wrong. Derrick had put up with a lot of things in their past. She just hoped their relationship could survive this one.

Chapter 3

Sasha nursed a glass of rum punch while listening to the sounds of Flo Rida. She stood against the wall and watched as a very muscular Bahamian man danced his way into the hearts of the women in the room. He grinned as they screamed and placed dollar bills into the elastic of his bright red briefs. By the end of the song, Dexter, the male dancer enlisted by the bridal party, was sitting on Bridget's lap. With one hand covering her eyes, she spanked his behind lightly with the other hand. The women in the room cheered as Dexter swiveled his hips and teased Bridget. She was embarrassed but managed to laugh through it.

Sasha laughed at her sister but secretly wished for a moment that she could slip out of the room and catch some fresh air. She'd been pinned up with these women since heading for the spa earlier in the day. They'd gone to Paradise Island and been pampered with massages, manicures, pedicures and fresh hairdos. Sasha's freshly shampooed hair had blown in the wind as they'd visited every boutique and retail shop on Bay Street. They'd grabbed a bite to eat at one of the local Caribbean grills and then rushed back to the resort for a quick change of clothes before preparing for the beachside rehearsal dinner.

At the rehearsal dinner, the tables had been arranged along the sand and adorned with white tablecloths, white tea light candles and seashells in square vases that were gathered as centerpieces. The scent from the fresh plumeria flowers danced in the wind. The rehearsal dinner had been planned just before sunset, and the reflection of the beautiful colors was illuminated against the water. As contemporary jazz played and waves crashed against the shore, Sasha glanced across the table at Vince. He wore a white linen shirt with shorts to match. Holding a glass of wine in his hand, he chitchatted with the other groomsmen. He caught her watching and she quickly turned away, pretending to say something to her mother, who had been seated right next to her.

"They did a good job with the decorations," she said.

"Everything is just so beautiful." Her mother smiled.

"Yes, it is." She glanced at Vince again, and he raised his glass to her. She gave him a soft smile.

"I'm glad that you're finally taking a much-needed vacation, Sasha. You work too hard."

Here it comes, Sasha thought. Conversations with her mother were always strained. They always turned to Sasha's career and how she worked too hard or how she made bad decisions in her personal life. Sasha wished her mother would be proud of her accomplishments, but instead she diminished them. Sasha wanted so badly for her mother to be proud of her.

"I enjoy my job, Mother."

Charlotte Winters looked for something else to complain about. "What is this I hear about you leaving after the wedding?"

"My office is having a retreat in Savannah. I need to be there."

"Your sister is getting married. You need to be here."

"I am here, Mother."

"I mean for the entire event. Not just the nuptials. There was a lot of effort put into planning this weekend, and it seems that you're blowing it off."

"I'm not blowing it off. I'll be here for the most important part—the vows," explained Sasha.

"You're taking this career of yours way too seriously. You're just like your father. Never know when to quit." Charlotte took a sip of her wine.

Sasha had taken a sip of her own wine, and she enjoyed the ambiance for a while. The last thing she wanted to do was get into it with her mother. Their views about life were as different as night and day, and she typically avoided any discussion with her mother. It was a losing battle.

She watched as Vince stood and offered a toast and well-wishes to the bride and groom. She followed suit with well-wishes of her own. After the delectable Bahamian meal was served, it was back to the condo for yet another change of clothes. Bridget's bachelorette party soon followed.

Sasha hadn't had a moment to herself since arriving in the Bahamas, and she needed one desperately. As soon as Dexter had everyone's attention again, Sasha slipped out of the suite, closing the door gently behind her. She rushed down the sidewalk, making a clean escape. She thought she'd retreat to her condo for a nice long bubble bath, and then maybe a walk on the beach. The night was beautiful—the moon lit up the sky with its brightness. She'd worn skinny jeans and high heels to Bridget's party but wished she'd opted for a bikini top, a colorful sarong and flat sandals instead. She removed the heels from her aching feet and felt the warmth of the pavement against her toes.

"I would never have guessed you to be a country girl." The voice behind her startled her. She turned to find Vince leaning against a palm tree, the neck of a bottle of Heineken between his fingers.

"Excuse me?" she said.

"Walking barefoot is what country girls do," he explained. "I thought you were a city girl."

"I grew up in the city, but my parents are definitely from the country," she said. He was not exactly the breath of fresh air she'd needed all night.

"I thought you were at your bachelorette party, getting your groove on." He grinned that grand piano of a smile.

"I've had enough fun for one night. What about you? Shouldn't you be somewhere sticking one-dollar bills into the thong of some overdeveloped Bahamian hoochie?"

Vince laughed this time. She liked his laugh—it was hearty and real. She couldn't help noticing how handsome he looked in his designer jeans and silk shirt.

"I've never heard it put that way, but I'm sure the young lady that they hired is getting plenty of dollar bills without me." He took a sip of his beer. "Where you headed?"

"To my condo for a long bath," said Sasha.

"Ooh, sounds wonderful." He smiled. "Any chance I could convince you to have a drink with me first?"

"Hmm, I don't know. I've had enough wine and rum punch to carry me through the night."

"One drink," Vince pressed.

"Just one?" Sasha was close to conceding.

"Just one."

As much as Sasha wanted to play hard to get, she couldn't. She'd secretly hoped that she would bump into Vince. He'd cluttered her thoughts all day—the intoxicating smell of his cologne, his eyes and that smile had haunted her. She'd wondered how he was spending his day while she was being pampered with the girls. Had he driven his rented Mercedes along the streets of Nassau, sightseeing? Was he a shopper? A fisherman? Did he play golf? Perhaps that was the *thing* that Vince and her father had in common. She'd found herself wondering these things and couldn't for the life of her understand why.

Vince helped Sasha climb onto a stool at the poolside bar.

He asked, "What are you having?"

"I'm a wine girl," she said, and then turned to the bartender, "Your house Chardonnay, please."

"A Black Russian for me, Jake," said Vince, calling the bartender by name.

"What is a Black Russian, anyway?" Sasha asked.

"Vodka and Kahlua," Vince explained.

"Is it good?"

"It's an interesting drink, with many variations." He raised his glass after Jake set the drink in front of him. "This is a Black Russian. Add cola, and it becomes a Dirty Black Russian. Add ginger ale, and you have a Brown Russian. Add a touch of Guinness beer, and you have a Smooth Black Russian." His voice was sultry as those last three words rolled off his tongue. *Smooth Black Russian.*

"Okay, I get it."

"You should try one."

"I'm not much of a drinker."

"You're on vacation. Let go of your inhibitions. Live a little," Vince suggested. "Jake, give the lady a Brown Russian."

"How do you know I wouldn't like a Smooth Black Russian? Or perhaps a dirty one?"

"You don't strike me as smooth or dirty," teased Vince.

"I beg your pardon. You don't know me like that." Sasha giggled and took a long sip of her wine.

"You're right. I don't know you as well as I'd like to," Vince said. "How does one break through that hard exterior of yours—that shield that you put up for the world?"

"I don't have a shield!" Sasha argued. "You don't know anything about me."

"I know that you're a workaholic, and you'd rather be somewhere other than here right now."

He was wrong. She was exactly where she wanted to be at the moment.

"My firm is hosting a retreat on Tybee Island this weekend, and it's imperative that I be there. Only…my sister is getting married, and I can't be in two places at one time."

"And your career is hanging in the balance because you're not there. And there's some other hotshot attorney that's threatening to steal your spot," Vince stated sarcastically.

"How'd you know that?" Sasha asked as Jake placed a Brown Russian in front of her.

Completely ignoring her question, Vince asked, "Who's your rival? Some young, blond-haired, blue-eyed little geek who graduated Yale or Harvard at the top of his class?"

"No, actually *she* has brown hair and brown eyes, and graduated from UCLA. And I taught her everything she knows."

"And now she's your rival? I'd say she's not very appreciative," Vince said. "She's at that retreat right now, isn't she?"

"Rubbing noses with clients I should be rubbing noses with," said Sasha as she took a sip of her Brown Russian. It didn't make her cringe as she suspected it would, and before long she'd finished almost half. "What about you, Vince? What would you be doing right now if you weren't here?"

"Let me see…" Vince checked his watch. "You mean at this very moment?"

"Yes, at this very moment."

"Right now I'd be sipping a cup of something hot trying to get my voice back after running up and down the sidelines of a basketball court, yelling at the top of my lungs because my kids were losing. Or because they were winning."

"So you have children." It was more a statement than a question. A resolution. She suddenly felt a sense of disappointment. Either he was married, divorced or had a baby's mama, and any way that spelled trouble. That is, if she were interested in him romantically. Which she wasn't.

"Yes, I have fifteen children." Vince grinned as Sasha's eyes grew bigger. "I coach a youth league coed basketball team. And they had a game tonight."

"Wow, a youth team. You must love children." She sighed with relief, and then her heart warmed at the thought.

"They are the most honest people on the face of the earth. You don't have to pretend with them. You just have to protect them. And teach them to take care of their teeth." Vince polished off his Black Russian and raised his glass for Jake to bring him another.

"Their teeth, huh?" Sasha asked, and then she remembered her conversation with Bridget earlier. "You're a dentist."

"Yes." Vince grinned. "A pediatric dentist."

"Oh." Sasha covered her mouth with her hand, wondering if he'd already inspected her teeth.

"Don't worry. You have a nice set of teeth." It was as if he'd read her mind. "I've already checked them out."

"You are…something else." Sasha smiled and shook her head. She found herself more engaged than she wanted to be.

She raised her glass to alert Jake that she needed another Brown Russian, and before long she'd polished off three. Suddenly Vince's jokes became outrageously funny, and Sasha found herself laughing long and hard—and loudly. Vince pulled his chair around closer to Sasha, until she could feel his breath on her neck. His cologne crept its way into her nostrils.

"You smell wonderful," she whispered.

His lips pressed themselves against hers, and his tongue teased the inside of her mouth. Whatever good sense she had was out the window as Vince took her to a new level of delight. His huge hand palmed her head and pulled her closer, and she wondered what that hand would feel like on her breast and even between her thighs. It had been a very long time since she'd even been kissed by a man. With his gentle touch, Vince had awakened every sensation in her and she got lost in the moment. She simply got lost.

As the bright sunshine beamed through her window and crept across her face, Sasha slowly and reluctantly opened her eyes. Her head was pounding—the alcohol had proved to be a more powerful force than she thought. She groaned, regretting every Brown Russian that she'd indulged in with a man whom she barely knew. It was her sister's wedding day, and she knew she wouldn't have the luxury of recovering from her awful hangover. She needed to meet the other girls for hair and makeup at eleven. And the nuptials were scheduled to take place at noon. As much as it pained her, she needed to know what time it was, and she slowly turned her aching head to look at the digital clock on the nightstand.

With a loud shriek, she jumped out of bed.

"What are you doing here?" she asked Vince, who was nestled beneath the crisp white sheets in her bed. She grabbed her thick bathrobe from the chair and wrapped it around her naked body. "Oh, my God! Did you…did we?"

"Did we make love?" Vince was calm and didn't move.

"Did we have sex?"

"Having sex sounds so cheap and lustful. Making love sounds so much more passionate." Vince smiled and sat up in bed.

"Oh, no, this is bad. This is so bad. I never sleep with guys on the first date. Was this even a date?"

"I'd say it was a date," he mused.

"This isn't funny, Vince. We barely even know each other." Sasha plopped down into the chair. Her hands covered her face as she contemplated her predicament.

A loud knock on the door shook her from her thoughts.

"Sasha!" Her mother's voice wasn't one that she needed to hear at the moment. "Sasha, honey, open up! It's Mom."

"Shh," Sasha mouthed to Vince as she pressed her index finger against her lips.

Charlotte knocked again. "Sasha, are you in there? You have hair and makeup in thirty minutes."

Sasha's heart pounded while her mother knocked two more times. She hoped Charlotte hadn't talked house-keeping into giving her a spare key to the room. Vince stood and slipped his jeans on and buckled his belt. Sasha took in the curve of his bare chest and arms. She wondered if those arms had held her hips steady in the middle of the night or if they'd wrapped themselves around her naked body just hours before.

Sasha sighed with relief when her mother stopped knocking. She was gone.

"You have to go," she told Vince. "If I know Charlotte Winters, she'll be back. And she won't knock next time."

Vince buttoned his silk shirt and slipped his loafers on his feet. He walked over to Sasha, pulled her up from the chair and wrapped his strong arms around her. When he pressed his lips against hers, she didn't pull away. Her open mouth welcomed his tongue. He stopped in midkiss, leaving her longing for more.

"See you at the altar," he said and then exited her condo.

Chapter 4

With fingers intertwined, Sasha held on tightly to the small bouquet of mandarin-colored lilies. The small hotel conference room had been transformed into a quaint little wedding chapel. Although the couple was supposed to exchange vows on the beach, the wedding had unexpectedly been moved inside because of a few little sprinkles of rain. Her sister looked as if she'd just stepped out of the pages of *Black Bride & Groom* magazine, with her chic and stylish strapless Vera Wang gown and its flowing train. Bridget was a picture of beauty as their father escorted her down the aisle, delivering her to her husband-to-be. Her hair flowing against her shoulders and her makeup flawless, she looked happier than Sasha had ever seen her. Derrick looked proud as he awaited her arrival.

Sasha stole a glance at the best man, and he gave her a sly grin and a wink. The night before had been a blur, and she struggled with the thought that she'd slept with a man whom she barely knew. She wondered what it had been like. She didn't know. All she remembered after four Brown Russians was a romantic walk along the beach before ultimately passing out. Vince must've carried her to her condo, because she couldn't for the life of her remember walking there. He'd obviously undressed her and took advantage of her limp and helpless body.

She glared at him. He looked confused as to why she looked at him that way. He offered an apologetic smile. She rolled her eyes and directed her attention to the bride and groom and the gray-haired Bahamian minister who read Scriptures from a tattered Bible. She would simply ignore him for the remainder of the afternoon, and soon she'd be on a plane headed for Savannah. She would never have to see Vince again if she played her cards right. She could successfully avoid him for the rest of her life, except for those awkward moments when they both would be invited to Derrick and Bridget's home at the same time. She'd cross that bridge when she got to it, but for now, Vince Sullivan did not exist in her world.

Avoiding him wasn't as easy as she expected, especially when he decided to unexpectedly grab her by the waist and whisk her onto the dance floor at the reception.

"Are you avoiding me, Sasha Winters?" he asked as they slow-danced to Beyonce's version of Etta James's "At Last."

"Yes," she said.

"Why?"

"Because you're a predator," she growled. "You took advantage of me while I was in a vulnerable state."

"You were drunk, girl. Plain and simple," he said.

"And I'll have you know, you tried to take advantage of me!"

"What? You're insane." Sasha lowered her voice and then looked around the room. The bride and groom danced cheek to cheek just a few feet away.

"Am I?"

"Yes!" she shouted and then looked around at the questioning eyes in the room—namely Bridget, who gave her a look that said *what's going on with you two?* She lowered her voice. "Yes, you are insane if you think that I took advantage of you."

"You're right. It was the other way around," he whispered in her ear, his breath warm and gentle against her earlobe. "I took you back to your room, slowly undressed you. I stood there for a moment…took in the beauty of your sexy naked body. Your breasts were so round and firm and plump. And your nipples…they were so hard. I placed them between my lips one at a time…"

Sasha found herself in a trance under the sound of his voice. She should've been mortified by the things he was saying, but she was all but.

"Then I took you. And you felt so good, baby," he whispered. "I would love to do it again…and again… and again."

She wanted to kiss his sexy lips, right there in the middle of that dance floor. As his huge, soft hand caressed the small of her bare back, she imagined him *taking her*—and wondered again what it had been like, because she certainly couldn't remember one single detail of it.

"If you'll excuse me, I have to go," she said. "I have to get packed for my flight."

"Your flight?" Vince asked.

"Yes, you know…on a jet. That huge piece of metal that's going to take me away from here to Savannah, Georgia, in just a few hours."

"So you think that you're catching a flight in a few hours?"

"I know so," Sasha said confidently.

"I think you should come with me." Vince grabbed Sasha's elbow and led her out of the hotel's ballroom and to the front of the building.

Sasha peered out the window and noticed that it was pitch-black outside. It was pouring rain with an occasional roar of thunder.

"Oh, my God," she whispered to herself, and then pulled her iPhone from her glittery silver purse. She tried calling the airline but wasn't able to get through—the call failed. Rushing over to the hotel's concierge, she asked, "Can I use your phone to check on my flight? I'm supposed to catch a red-eye out of here at eleven."

"Ma'am, I'm sorry, but our phone lines are down right now. We're not able to get an outside line," said the dark gentleman in his Bahamian accent. "And you won't be catching a flight out tonight. All flights have been canceled due to the storm."

"Are you sure?" she asked.

The concierge directed her attention to the television anchored in the corner of the wall. The newscaster's mouth was moving but with the television on mute, and Sasha couldn't make out what he was saying.

"Can you turn that up, please?" she asked the hotel's reservation agent.

The woman obliged and the newscaster's voice echoed throughout the lobby. "All flights leaving Nassau's L. Pindling Airport have been canceled this evening."

Sasha wanted to rewind the newscast, just to see if she'd misheard. She paced the floor, unsure of what to do. She tried her phone again, wanting to get through to the airline just to see for herself. She wanted to hear them say it personally—that her flight had been canceled. Spending another night in the Bahamas was not in the plans. However, she wasn't completely disappointed. There was something about the handsome man who sat across the room watching her every move. His presence sent her hormones into a frenzy. And spending an extra night in the Bahamas might help her to understand exactly what it was she was feeling inside.

Chapter 5

Vince sat in a chair across the room and watched her, admired her. With his fingers intertwined, he made a slow circular motion with his thumbs. He took in her beautiful chestnut face and couldn't remember ever seeing a prettier shade of brown. He traced her round lips with his eyes and imagined kissing them again. He'd watched her earlier at the ceremony as she'd made her way down the aisle. She'd taken his breath away. The satin dress had clung to her hips. He wondered how beautiful she would have looked in the ivory gown that her sister wore. He didn't know very much about Sasha Winters, except that she was a workaholic and a bit self-absorbed.

He remembered the day she rammed her car into his at Derrick's condo. She'd been so preoccupied and careless. She'd ruined the custom paint on his car, but it didn't matter much. It had been painted by a good friend of his who owned a body shop in Atlanta. He would've touched it up for him for little to nothing. He'd given Sasha a hard time about it only because he felt she'd blown it off as unimportant. He'd been angry and had used the incident to teach her a lesson. He'd been interested in her the first time he saw her, though, but soon realized that she was in a relationship with someone else. Not that he was really ready for a relationship at the time. He was still sowing his wild oats, so to speak.

However, his days of being with multiple women were long over. In college, it had been a challenge among his friends and him to see who could bed the most women and share every detail with each other. As an athlete, Vince didn't have to work very hard to win the challenge; women often chased him and became more accessible than he desired. They'd robbed him of the chase, and therefore caused him to become bored with the opposite sex. He wanted to be the chaser, and most women didn't allow him to do that. Even well past his college days, and as he worked in his current profession, he had to fight off the advances of the single mothers who brought their children into his dental office. His admirers included a few married ones too.

Seeing Sasha in the Bahamas had instantly piqued his interest again. She'd been the first woman who'd captured his attention in a very long time. Her fiery attitude captivated him, and he found himself thinking about her when she wasn't around. He thought of last night and how he'd carried her to her condo. She'd vomited all over the sandy beach and then passed out in his arms. Once inside her condo, she'd awakened and began to undress, begging him to do the same. He refused, but she was persistent.

"Come on," she'd whispered in a slur, "what are you afraid of?"

"We can't," he'd whispered back, "as much as I'd like to…I can't."

She'd grabbed the buckle of his belt and struggled with it. Vince had grabbed her hands.

"Can you just hold me then?" she'd asked.

That is exactly what he'd done—held his strong arms around her naked body for most of the night, his chin resting upon the top of her head long after she'd fallen asleep. It felt good there. He felt as if he'd been her protector; he hoped that she'd felt safe in his arms. His manhood had grown hard and rested against the small of her back. He could easily have made love to her right then and there, but he didn't want it like that. He wanted her—all of her and not just her body.

He glanced over at Sasha as she paced the floor in the hotel lobby and continued to try and reach an outside line. Finally she looked defeated and helpless. He wished he could fix things and make things right for her. It was what he did for the women in his life—his mother and younger sister. He took care of them.

After his father's tragic heart attack, Vince became the man of the house at seventeen. So taking care of people had become second nature for him. He found himself doing it without thinking and driving his younger sister crazy in the process. Dating had become nearly impossible for Gabrielle Sullivan, and she told him so every chance she got. Having an older brother who thought he was her father had made her upbringing almost unbearable. He couldn't wait to protect Sasha just as he had the other women in his life. If she'd give him half a chance, he'd take care of her for life. He wished he could make her problems at the moment disappear. However, truth be told, he reveled in the thought that she would be spending another night on the islands.

"Can I help?" he finally asked.

She looked at him, grinned and said, "Not unless you have a private jet that could get me to Savannah."

"Unfortunately, I didn't bring my private jet to the Bahamas. But I'll be happy to take you back to my condo for a nightcap."

"I just bet you would," she said sarcastically and then tried making a call on her iPhone again. After which, she approached him and lowered her voice to whisper, "The last time we drank together we ended up doing things that I can't even remember doing."

"We did, didn't we?" Vince mused. "I remember quite well."

"You're a pig," Sasha growled, "and no, I will not be joining you in your room for a nightcap or anything else for that matter."

"Suit yourself." Vince stood. "You know where to find me if you need me."

As he walked away, he thought of the look on Sasha's face. She was appalled that he would suggest that she join him in his condo. He was very attracted to her—no doubt about it, but she was a tough one. She wasn't like the women he'd dated in the past. In the past, he'd be making excuses as to why he couldn't spend time with someone. He'd be avoiding or ducking and dodging. But not with Sasha. She intrigued him.

In his condo, Vince stripped down to his boxers and dress socks. His arms were mountains of chiseled muscle, and his legs were strong from playing football and running track in high school and college. Even now, he was a runner. Just this morning, he'd run along the beach after abruptly leaving Sasha's room. Running relaxed him. It kept him balanced, especially during a time when he felt a little out of balance. Sasha did that to him—she caused him to think he could actually have a future with her, and he barely even knew her.

He placed ice cubes into a glass and poured scotch over them. After stirring the drink with his index finger, he stood in front of the glass patio door and watched the rain as it danced across the concrete outside. Darkness covered the sky, except for the occasional flash of lightning. He wondered if Sasha was still pacing the floor in the lobby or if she'd taken to walking back to the United States. The sound of Wayman Tisdale's bass guitar bounced against the walls as he listened to jazz on his iPod from its docking station. He had a soft spot for jazz, contemporary and classic. Sometimes he enjoyed Coltrane or Miles Davis, and even a few jazz fusion artists like Michael Franks.

He barely heard the light tap on the door, but he slipped on a pair of sweatpants before seeing who it was. Peeping through the hole, he smiled as he watched Sasha become restless and check her watch. Just the sight of her made his heart beat faster. She had changed into a pair of jeans and a bright green T-shirt. He took in the curve of her hips and the way the snug T-shirt hugged her breasts.

Swinging the door open, he said, "I thought you'd be halfway back to the States by now."

"Very funny," she said. "The electricity in my condo went out, and I just wondered…"

"…if you could borrow some of my mine?"

"I wondered if yours was out too."

"Nah, I have lights." Vince smiled. "And yes, you can borrow some. Please come in."

"I was wondering if I could charge the battery on my phone." She held her phone and charger in the air. "Completely dead."

"No problem."

"I hate to impose," she stated apologetically, "and I would ask my sister, but she's probably somewhere making babies with her new hubby."

"Probably," Vince agreed. "Why don't you step inside?"

Sasha stepped into Vince's condo and lingered near the door.

"Make yourself at home. There's an outlet right here in the living area. Give it here and I'll plug it in for you."

She handed him her iPhone and he plugged it into the wall next to the lamp. She looked around, assessing the place.

"Your room is different. Bigger."

"Different, yes. It's not much bigger than your place, though. One bedroom, just like yours."

"No really, your living area is bigger. And your kitchen seems more spacious."

"I think you just see things a bit differently." Vince moved in closer to Sasha. So much so that he could smell the mint in her mouth.

Soon, her back was against the door.

"And I think you're rude," she responded.

"I think you came by here to see me to take me up on my invitation for a nightcap." Vince smiled. "You could've gone anywhere on this property to charge your phone, but you chose here. As a matter of fact, I don't think that your electricity went out at all. I think you just needed an excuse to come to my room and seduce me."

"Really?" She smiled, didn't admit or deny.

"And furthermore, I think you want me to kiss your

lips right now." He leaned in closer, tried to brush his lips against hers, but she placed her long, skinny index finger against them.

"What do you think you're doing?" she asked.

"Trying to kiss you."

"Who said that I wanted you to kiss me?" she asked.

"I just thought…"

"I don't know what you thought, Mr. Sullivan, but—" she slipped away from the corner "—I just came to charge my phone."

The patter of the rain outside his window sounded like music—intermingling with the sound of jazz playing on his iPod.

"Right," he said, and went to the kitchen. He grabbed a beer from his refrigerator and held it in the air. "Would you like one?"

"Sure." She slid into the green chair in the corner of the room.

He twisted the cap off the beer and handed her the bottle. "So, when did you first realize that you were attracted to me?" he asked.

"Excuse me? Who said I was attracted to you at all?"

"You are." He smiled. "You can't resist my charm, and you know it."

"You're very arrogant," she stated, "and presumptuous."

Ignoring her statement, he said, "I was attracted to you the moment I saw you at Bridget's birthday party two years ago. You wore this gorgeous red dress with these big silver doohickeys in your ear." He remembered because he hadn't been able to take his eyes off her the entire evening. "What is it with women and big earrings?"

"Um, I don't know."

Vince could tell that she was surprised by his revelation that he'd been attracted to her for a long time, and he realized that he'd said too much—given her too much. He walked toward the patio door while changing the subject. "Man, it's really coming down out there."

"I usually love the rain—when it's not altering my plans." She stood and walked over to the patio door to stand next to him. "I remember sitting on my parents' porch when I was a little girl, watching the rain, wishing it would stop so that Bridget and I could go out and play."

"Why didn't you just go play in it?"

"Who does that?"

"Me! And every other child in America." Vince smiled. "You mean you've never played in the rain?"

"On purpose?" she asked. "No, can't say that I have."

"What?" He gave her a look of shock. "You have to play in the rain at least once in your life, Sasha. It's one of those things you have to do before you die. Where's your audacity, your sense of adventure?"

"Who has time for adventure?"

"You make time for adventure!" He slid the patio door open then grabbed her by the hand. "Let's go."

"Go where?" she asked as he pulled her along and through the patio doors.

"We're going to play in the rain!"

"You mean in the storm?"

"Yes! Whatever you want to call it," Vince stated.

"What about my hair?" Sasha shrieked.

"Your hair?" Vince asked. "Boy, you really are a black woman, aren't you?"

"Yes, I am. And I just got my hair done yesterday! And it wasn't cheap."

Before she could say another word, Vince had pulled

her out into the rain and the two of them had rushed down the sidewalk. They were the only two souls outside, and Vince hoped that he hadn't overstepped his bounds with Sasha. Not everyone enjoyed his carefree attitude and spontaneity. He sighed with relief when he heard her burst with laughter. They laughed together as the heavy raindrops pounded upon their heads—saturating Sasha's freshly done coiffure. She didn't even seem to mind after a while. He wrapped his strong arms around her from behind and squeezed her tightly. Her warmth felt good against his chest, and he could've stayed there forever.

Vince spotted an open door to the hotel's kitchen.

"Let's dip into here," he stated.

"What?" Sasha hesitated. "We can't go in there."

Vince peeked inside to make sure the coast was clear before pulling Sasha in. They quickly moved across the tile flooring in the kitchen—past huge stainless steel sinks and a commercial refrigerator.

"What are you two doing?" asked a heavyset Bahamian woman wearing a crisp white chef's jacket.

"We're sorry, we just got a little turned around," Vince lied and started walking back toward the door.

"A little turned around, eh? Come." She smiled, and then stated in her Bahamian accent, "Since you're here, I want you to taste some-ting."

They followed the woman through the industrial kitchen and to a small table in the corner.

"I'm Clara, by the way," she said. "And you are?"

Vince spoke first. "I'm Vince and this is Sasha."

"Married?"

"We're just friends," Sasha quickly stated.

"Just friends, eh?" Clara asked as if she was skeptical about it.

Clara's Bahamian features were strong; her face was a creamy, flawless dark brown. She reminded Vince of a woman he called Big Mama when he was growing up—his grandmother, whom he'd loved dearly. She'd passed away just a few years after he'd graduated dental school. It had felt as if his heart would never heal; Big Mama had been one of his favorite people.

"Sit," Clara ordered and then walked over to the stove. She grabbed two bowls and filled them with rice and peas, then placed a bowl and fork in front of each of them. "I want you to taste my peas and rice. Tell me if you like."

Vince didn't hesitate to pick up his fork and dig in. He loved Bahamian dishes and was no stranger to peas and rice.

"Delicious!" he exclaimed with a full mouth.

"Don't talk with your mouth full, child," the woman scolded. "Hasn't anyone ever told you dat?"

He chewed and swallowed before saying, "Yes, ma'am. Sorry."

"I'm glad you like." Clara smiled and looked at Sasha. "What about you, child?"

"It's surprisingly good," said Sasha. "I don't usually like peas, but this is good."

"Here." Clara walked over to the stove, brought back a pan with fish in it. She placed fish on each of their plates.

She hadn't bothered to ask if they'd eaten or if they even wanted to eat. She just placed food in front of them and demanded. The two of them ate like savages, and before they were allowed to leave the table, Clara had placed a johnnycake on each of their plates.

"Miss Clara, this is so good," said Sasha. "Where did you learn to cook like this?"

"From my mother. Generations of cooks in our family."

"Well, you were taught well," said Vince.

"So what is the story with you two, eh?" Clara asked.

"What do you mean?" asked Sasha.

"Are you married, engaged, fooling around…what?" She folded her arms across her ample chest.

Vince and Sasha looked at each other.

"Just friends," Sasha stated again.

"Barely even know each other," Vince added.

"He's not even my type," said Sasha while stuffing her mouth with a huge chunk of johnnycake.

"Well, what is your type, honey?" asked Clara. "Because he's as handsome as he wanna be."

"Thank you, Miss Clara." Vince smiled. "And yes, Sasha, what exactly is your type?"

"Uh…well…I don't know," Sasha stumbled. "It's not like I'm looking."

"She's absolutely my type, Miss Clara," Vince said. "She's beautiful, intelligent, career-minded. She's got those nice baby-bearing hips."

Clara and Vince laughed heartily. Sasha frowned.

"Ha-ha, very funny," said Sasha, who didn't find his comment the least bit amusing.

"It's clear that you have a *ting* for each other," said Clara. "I remember when I met my Roger. He was tall and handsome, and so full of life. I loved him instantly, but I didn't want him to know that right away. I wanted him to work for it, ya know?"

"And did he work for it?" Vince asked with a smile.

"He most certainly did." Clara smiled. "And thirty-five years later, there's still plenty of love."

Vince pondered on Clara's comments about her husband having to work for her love. He wondered how long and how hard he'd have to work to win Sasha's heart. He watched her as she ran her fingertips across her damp hair, trying to make the best of it. He felt guilty for making her run in the rain and ruin her high-priced hairdo.

Clara began to gather the soiled dishes and carry them over to the commercial sink. She filled the sink with hot soapy water and washed the dishes by hand.

"Can we help?" asked Sasha.

"No. You kids go do whatever it was you were on your way to do."

Sasha stood and looked for a clean, dry towel. She found two and tossed Vince one.

"I'll rinse and you dry," she told Vince.

"I don't need any help," Clara insisted.

"It's okay. We don't mind," said Sasha.

Sasha and Vince laughed heartily as Clara told stories about growing up in Nassau and about her dysfunctional relatives. She told stories of her courtship with Roger, and on a more serious note, how he was dying of cancer. The doctors had already done all that they could do, and Roger had been sent home to spend his last days with those he loved the most—Clara and their golden retriever, Dixie. Clara was never able to give Roger any children, so Dixie had been the next-best thing. She'd been a part of their family for many years.

When Clara realized that the discussion about Roger had left a feeling of gloom in the room, she changed the subject. "Well, you two better get going. The rain has eased a bit."

"Thank you for dinner, Miss Clara. It was delicious." Vince kissed Clara's cheek. "I would love the recipe for those peas and rice."

Clara pulled a small notepad and pen out of the

pocket of her chef's jacket. "Give me your address and I will mail it to you."

Vince took the notepad and jotted down his address. Clara reciprocated and wrote hers down, as well. "I expect an invitation to the wedding when the two of you get married."

"Us?" asked Sasha.

"Yes, you." Clara grinned and then walked over to the door and opened it. "Now, go. I have plenty of work to do. I can't be bothered with you two all night."

Vince and Sasha walked toward the door. Sasha gave Clara a hug and then the two of them went out into the night. The huge door closed behind them.

"She was nice," said Sasha.

"She was." Vince grabbed her hand, intertwining his fingers with hers.

Just as Clara knew instantly that she loved Roger, Vince knew he could possibly—very possibly—love Sasha.

Chapter 6

They returned to the condo, and as soon as the door closed, Vince pulled Sasha into his arms.

He breathed in the smell of her perfume or bath oils. He wasn't sure which, but he loved her scent. Her arms wrapped themselves around his neck and he hungrily kissed her lips. His fingertips caressed her neck and then danced across her shoulder. He palmed her round breast through her cotton shirt and stroked her nipple with the tips of his fingers. With one quick move he had lifted her shirt and unsnapped her bra. His hand caressed her bare breast. The sensation of touching her bare skin sent a wave of electricity through him. He couldn't quite remember needing anyone so much.

As jazz played on his iPod, he lifted Sasha and she wrapped her legs around his waist. He carried her to his bedroom and gently placed her on the bed. After softly running his fingertips over her stomach, he found his way down to unsnap her jeans, and he removed them too. He noticed the chill bumps that danced across her skin and wondered if she was cold or nervous—or both.

"Are you okay?" he whispered.

She silently nodded a yes.

"Just relax," he urged.

Vince removed his shirt and tossed it onto the chair across the room. Sasha slowly caressed his chest with her soft hands. He removed his sweatpants and rested his heavy body on top of Sasha's small frame.

"I want you," he stated softly but urgently, "but if you're not ready, we can wait."

"I don't want to wait," Sasha whispered.

And with that, Vince moved forward. He grabbed his wallet from the nightstand and searched for the condom that he'd placed inside for safekeeping. His lips found hers again, and he began to kiss her deeply. He planted a trail of kisses on her lips, her chin and then her neck. His lips traced the roundness of her breasts and then made their way down to her navel. When he kissed the insides of her thighs, Sasha moaned.

His lips made their way back up to Sasha's, and then he gently placed himself inside her. His hips moved to the sound of the music as the two of them made a song of their own. He found peace with her. His heart and body felt things that he couldn't quite understand. Making love to this woman had him rethinking everything in his life; rearranging everything. He knew he wanted her in every possible way—physically, emotionally and intellectually.

With her arms stretched wide and her palms facing the ceiling, he rested his hands in hers and collapsed on top of her. He didn't want to move. He wanted to lie there forever—for as long as she'd allow him to. He'd been to the mountaintop and back and knew that she'd been there too. He could see it in her eyes—they told him everything he wanted to know. He rolled over and then pulled her close to him and wrapped his arms tightly around her.

"That was amazing," he said.

"Better than the other night?" she asked.

He was confused for a moment and then realized that she didn't know the details of their first encounter. "I have a confession." He smiled. "We didn't do anything the other night."

"Really?" she asked.

"You were too drunk. I took you to your room, undressed you and tucked you safely into bed."

"Then why were you in my bed?"

"Because you insisted on it. You had no clothes on, and you wanted me to take mine off, too. Asked me to do all kinds of things, but I resisted. I was the perfect gentleman."

"The perfect gentleman, huh?"

"Yes, I was."

"Why didn't you? I mean, most men would have jumped at the chance to take advantage of a drunk, naked woman begging him to do all sorts of things to her body. Who could resist?"

"I could resist. I wanted you to be aware of what you were doing. I wanted it to be consensual and beautiful."

"And was it consensual and beautiful this time?" Sasha's voice cracked at the thought of him wanting their lovemaking to be beautiful. She thought it was the sweetest thing he'd said since they met.

"More beautiful than anything I've experienced."

"Is this one of those vacation things…you know, woman meets this handsome man on a tropical island

and he ravishes her. Like a tropical fantasy or something, where they hook up, hit it and never hook up again. Kinda like a 'what happens in Vegas, stays in Vegas' sort of thing."

Vince grabbed Sasha's chin and forced her to look at him. Staring into her eyes, he said, "This was definitely not a hookup. I'd like to think it was the beginning of something very special."

And with that, Sasha's lips met his. Soon, her eyes grew heavy and began to close, and before long she was asleep. Vince watched as she took each quick breath, and then he held her close as she slept peacefully in his arms.

Chapter 7

The buffet table was a gorgeous tropical medley of orange tiger lilies, orchids, kale gingers and palm leaves. The presentation of pancakes, scrambled eggs, country sausage, grits and potatoes was grander than Sasha's usual breakfast. She usually just enjoyed a bagel from the corner pastry shop downtown and a Frappuccino from Starbucks. There had to be a million calories on that table just waiting to attack her hips.

She poured herself a tall glass of orange juice and contemplated grabbing a pancake or two—only because it had been so long since she'd indulged. She opted for the crepes instead, and a few potatoes.

"What happened to you last night, girlie? I looked for you all night," Bridget said as she approached her sister. "Are you okay?"

"Yeah, of course."

"I knocked on your door and called your room all night."

"I was, um…so tired." Sasha caught a quick glance at Vince. Bridget's friend Deja had him cornered near the bread table.

Sasha subtly maneuvered her body so that Bridget was shielding her, and she hoped he didn't see her. She hadn't had much time to evaluate her unexpected tryst with him and wasn't ready to discuss it. She was somewhat embarrassed, having given up the cookies so soon. It wasn't her style to sleep with a man so quickly, but it had been so long. He had awakened things in her that made her anxious. She broke every dating rule she'd ever known. The minute that she'd collected her clothing from the floor and slipped from his room in the wee hours of the morning, she knew that she'd made a mistake.

A conversation with him would be nothing less than awkward, she thought, as she attempted to hide behind her sister.

"I'm sorry about your flight last night, Sasquatch. I heard that everything was canceled because of the storm," said Bridget as she loaded her plate with more pancakes and potatoes than any one person should eat. "But selfishly…I'm kind of glad you're still here."

"Yeah, me too," Sasha had to admit. "It's really beautiful here. And I needed a vacation, even though I didn't want to admit it."

"You must've been really tired not to hear your mother banging on that door last night. I thought she was going to come unglued when you didn't answer. She called my room in a panic." Bridget giggled. "She'll definitely be looking for you bright and early this morning, sister."

"Yeah, I know." Sasha made a quick move toward the scrambled eggs when she saw Vince look her way.

"You sure you're okay? You're acting really goofy, girl."

"I'm fine." Sasha faked a smile and then changed the subject. "Did you have a good time with your new hubby last night?"

Bridget breathed in deeply and lowered her voice. "I couldn't even get into it."

Sasha hadn't expected a candid response about her sister's sexual escapades with her new husband. She was simply making conversation.

"I was so cranky and bloated. I lied and told him I was on my period," Bridget continued, despite the horrified look on Sasha's face. "He was so mad! But like I told him, there will be plenty of time for sex another time."

"Bridget, it was your wedding night. You don't get a chance to redo that one."

"There will be other special occasions…birthdays, anniversaries. It's really not that serious."

"You're a piece of work." Sasha laughed. "My wedding night will be filled with fireworks and explosives!"

"Wasn't last night explosive enough?" Vince's voice was suddenly in her ear. His tone shook her. "I mean with all the lightning and thunder that went on. The storm was pretty intense, huh?"

"Yes it was," said Bridget. "Had me about ready to hide underneath the bed."

"What about you, Sasha? Were you afraid too…of the storm?" Vince asked, a sexy grin on his face. He was a delightful sight for such an early morning.

"No. I've, um…been in storms before. It was the usual…nothing to get all excited about." She gave Vince a smirk. Two could play his game. "Bridget, I'll chat with you later. I think I'm going to take my breakfast back to my room."

"Are you sure you want to do that?" asked Vince. "I have a table right over there on the terrace with an amazing view of the ocean. Why don't you join me?"

"I would love to, but I really have a lot of work to catch up on—a lot of emails to read. Maybe another time," Sasha said. "Bridget, I'll see you later."

"We're all going to ride Jet Skis this afternoon, Sasha, if the weather permits. You have to join us," said Bridget.

"You're getting on a Jet Ski?" Sasha asked with a raised eyebrow.

"I might," said Bridget, and then she remembered her condition. "And then again, I might not. But Paul's going. So maybe you two can hook up."

"Doubtful." Sasha gave her sister a half smile and then walked away.

"Sasha, I want to see you at the beach at noon," Bridget yelled.

Sasha kept walking, hoping Vince wasn't checking out her butt. She'd chosen a pair of khaki shorts that were a bit shorter than her usual taste. She'd purchased them on a whim—not truly intending on wearing them. But she had thrown them in her suitcase anyway. She felt sexy when she'd awakened this morning; felt more alive than she had in a long time. She couldn't deny that her encounter with Vince had awakened every one of her senses and left her wondering what he thought of it—of her.

The beach was beautiful. It seemed as if there had never been a storm, as if the waves hadn't collided against the shore with such fury. Jet Skis were revved up, and people were going out into the water in pairs. Dressed in bikinis, Bridget's bridesmaids hopped onto the backs of watercraft with whichever groomsman they fancied. Sasha had chosen a fuchsia-colored bikini with a colorful sarong tied around her waist. She had no interest in climbing onto the back of anybody's Jet Ski but thought she'd enjoy the beach anyway, maybe go for a swim. Perhaps she'd collect a few seashells hidden in the sand or relax on her beach towel while skimming through emails on her iPhone.

She spread her beach towel across the warm sand and removed her sarong. Bridget and Derrick strolled along the beach, their fingers intertwined. To the casual eye, they looked like happy newlyweds, but Sasha recognized the strain on her sister's face. They were arguing, probably about their wedding night failure. Sasha worried that her sister's marriage was already in trouble before it was given half a chance. She worried that Bridget would lose Derrick if she wasn't honest with him soon.

When she saw Vince approach the beach, she quickly pulled her *Essence* magazine out of her bag and buried her face in the pages of it. He shared a laugh with one of the other groomsmen, and Sasha couldn't help sneaking a peek every now and then. He wore black swimming trunks. His chest was bare and polished and his arms were a chiseled mass. She imagined those strong arms wrapped around her waist again, and those fingertips caressing every inch of her body as they had less than twenty-four hours before. His hands were soft and gentle, not calloused and rigid like those of most men she knew. She couldn't seem to contain her attraction to him, her need to watch every movement he made along the sand.

He looked her way and gave her a wink. She'd been caught staring and tried to play it off by sticking her nose in the magazine again. But it was too late. He was already making long strides in her direction. There wasn't any time to gather her belongings and make a mad dash for her condo, so instead she lifted her eyes and gave him a weak smile.

"Not doing the Jet Skis today?" He towered over her, blocking the sun from her eyes.

"No, not today," said Sasha.

"Can I convince you to go for a spin with me?"

"Hmm," she said thoughtfully, "probably not."

"Oh, come on. I'm a safe driver, and it would be so much fun." He smiled and reached for her hand. "Please?"

She placed her hand in his and he pulled her up. She dropped the magazine onto the beach towel. She followed Vince's eyes as he took in the sight of her body in the bikini. He'd been so intent he hadn't even noticed her watching him. As the two of them moved toward the water hand in hand, inquisitive eyes followed them. Sasha knew they'd be the talk of the wedding party before night's end.

She stood by as Vince paid the young Jet Ski owner and received instructions about safety in the water. Vince tightened his life jacket and then helped Sasha with hers. He was close enough to kiss her, and his touch excited her. After he snapped the life jacket snugly around her, she followed him into the water. She hopped onto the back of the watercraft and tightly held on to Vince's waist. She took in the scent of his cologne and the feel of his back against her chest, even though they were wearing life jackets. She still felt comfortable there, as if their bodies belonged together. Before she could finish her thought, the Jet Ski barreled across the water at a high level of speed, and Sasha found herself holding on for dear life. The faster Vince drove the Jet Ski, the tighter she held on—her face smashed against him. As they climbed each wave, unintentional bursts of laughter escaped her and she wondered where they came from. She couldn't help it. Laughter seemed to engulf her, and she couldn't control herself. Riding on the back of a Jet Ski with Vince was the most fun she'd had in a long time. She didn't even care that her hair was wet and windblown and she'd have to set aside extra prep time for the evening's cocktail party. If she decided to go.

In the middle of the ocean, Vince slowed the engine. He did small circles in the water, keeping the engine revved.

"You want to go for a swim?" he asked.

"Right now?"

"Yeah. Isn't that why you came to the beach? Or did you come just to lie on your beach towel and pretend to read your magazine?"

"I'll have you know I wasn't pretending. I came to the beach to relax," said Sasha. "And no, I do not want to go for a swim. I would actually like to go back to shore, if you don't mind."

"Well, I would like to go for a swim. At the count of three, we're going to switch places. You'll keep the engine running while I take a quick swim."

"Are you serious? I can't do that!" she shrieked.

"Sure you can. It's easy. Just scoot forward and place your hands on the handlebars. Behind the handlebars are levers that control your speed. Squeeze the levers to increase and decrease your speed. Make small circles in the water so the engine doesn't die. I won't be long, I promise." He jumped into the water, holding on to the Jet Ski until Sasha gained control of it. "Now move forward."

Sasha reluctantly moved up and placed her hands on the handlebars. She did as he instructed and started making circles in the water. Vince let go and started swimming, dipping his head underwater. He was crazy, Sasha thought. But she managed to make circles around him in the water as the engine of the Jet Ski revved underneath her.

"Oh, it feels good!" he yelled. "Wish you were in here too."

"You're crazy, you know that?" said Sasha.

"Yes, I know." Vince swam a few feet away from Sasha and back, and after a few laps he climbed back onto the Jet Ski and slid snugly behind her. "You can drive us back."

Nervously, Sasha changed the speed of the engine. She'd never driven a Jet Ski before. She'd never been on the back of one, for that matter.

"Just relax. Drive slowly and take control of the machine," Vince whispered.

After relaxing a bit, she increased the speed a tad more and headed toward the shore. His hands gently rested on her waist. He moved in closer, held her tighter and planted a trail of kisses against her neck.

"You are so sexy," he whispered in her ear, "and beautiful."

Her stomach did somersaults. As she moved closer to shore, Vince's fingertips wandered along the front of her life jacket and unsnapped it. She trembled when he touched her bare stomach and then gently moved up and caressed her breasts. She asked him to stop, but he didn't hear her. She'd only whispered it in her mind.

Yet, her body was screaming for him to continue. She wrapped her fingers tighter around the handlebars and leaned her back against Vince. He nibbled on her ear.

It was obvious that Sasha was the envy of every one of Bridget's friends as she parked the watercraft in the sand. Everyone looked on with inquisitive eyes. They wanted to know what was going on with these two, but they couldn't quite figure out how to ask.

Once the Jet Ski came to a complete stop, Vince hopped off and then helped Sasha climb from the craft. She removed her life jacket. Once she was able to feel her legs again, she headed toward her beach towel. All eyes were on the pair as Vince followed close behind.

"Well?" he simply said.

"Well what?" asked Sasha.

"I promised that it would be fun. Was it?"

"It was okay," Sasha lied. She wasn't ready to give him the satisfaction of being right.

"Just okay?" he asked. "Is that why you were laughing your head off the whole time?"

"It was nervous laughter." She gave him a slight grin.

She was keeping him at bay until she had things sorted out in her mind. Until she could make sense of what had taken place between them. And until she could place a label on what it was they were doing. If it was simply casual sex, then she wanted to call it what it was. If it was more, she needed to know that, too. Did she want it to be more? Did he? All these thoughts were racing through her mind as she packed her magazine and other items into her bag. She wrapped the sarong around her waist again and tied it.

"Okay, I had fun," she admitted. "Thanks for the ride."

"Will I see you at the cocktail party later?"

"I don't know, Vince. I mean, I have an early flight tomorrow morning and—" she placed the strap of her tote bag onto her shoulder and started to walk away "—I think we should just let things be."

Vince gently grabbed her arm. "Are you telling me there's no chemistry between us? That last night meant nothing to you?"

Sasha looked at his hand as if he'd overstepped his bounds by grabbing her. "I'm telling you that until I can sort out what took place last night, I think we should just let things be."

Vince released her arm and gave a slight nod in surrender. No other words were exchanged as Sasha began to trample through the warm sand and back toward the resort. She wanted him so badly. She knew it, and so did he. But placing her heart in a vulnerable state wasn't quite worth the risk. She didn't think she was in love with Vince, so moving past him should be easy. She'd fly back to Atlanta and go back to life as it was—he'd do the same, and they would both live happily ever after...separately. She wouldn't miss him. After all, you can't miss what you never had.

Her life was too complicated for a man right now, she thought. She was married to her career and there would be no place for him. She was comfortable, already set in her ways, and it would be too much of a hassle to switch things up now. She already had a rhythm, a groove. She wasn't willing to compromise. She'd compromised before, and look where it got her. She wasn't prepared for a brand-new heartache when the old one still lingered in her mind.

Sasha couldn't remember feeling like this about a man since her freshman year in college. Kevin had been her first real boyfriend. She'd been a late bloomer, a virgin, when she'd met him. She instantly fell in love with the Morehouse student who was fancied by many of the girls who attended Spelman, the all-girls college that was just across the courtyard. He was charming and had her floating in the clouds the moment they bumped into each other at the restaurant where he worked. She was instantly drawn to him.

"What are you doing tonight?" he'd asked.

"Studying," she'd said. "Midterms are coming up."

"Me too." He laughed. "But sometimes it's good to take a break from studying and have a little fun once in a while. You like poetry?"

"Love it."

"I dabble a little." He grinned. "I have a few pieces that I've written, and I do open mic at a little spot in Midtown. You wanna come check me out?"

Sasha thought for a moment. It was her first semester at Spelman, and so far she hadn't done anything fun besides attending the homecoming game with her friend and roommate, Robin.

"Can I bring my friend?"

"Of course." He scribbled the address on a piece of paper and handed it to her. "Show starts at eight."

"Okay, cool."

She knew that Robin would be reluctant to join her. Robin was serious about midterms. She partied hard in her off time but studied just as hard—and rarely went out in the middle of the week. It was the reason they got along so well; they shared the same ideas about their education. Both aspiring lawyers, they understood the importance of staying on course. They kept each other grounded. And even though Robin was more free-spirited than Sasha, they were more alike than they were different.

It was a tough sell, but Sasha had finally convinced Robin to tag along to the poetry session. They'd hopped into Sasha's old Chevy Malibu—the one her father had purchased for her high school graduation—and headed for the club in Midtown.

"We'll stay just a little while," Sasha said. "As soon as you're ready to go, we can go."

"You like this guy, huh?"

"He's cute."

"He must be something special—got Sasha Winters stepping out of her dorm in the middle of the week. And during midterms!"

"He seems nice." Sasha turned up the heat in the car and checked her makeup in the rearview mirror.

"He'd better have some good poetry, or I'm booing him," said Robin as she pulled her coat tighter.

"You wouldn't."

"I would, and you know it."

Sasha knew that Robin was serious. She was the most honest person she knew, and she didn't mind saying exactly what she thought. Sasha admired that trait yet wasn't always in the mood for Robin's honesty. Especially when it came to Kevin.

Sasha remembered the butterflies that danced in her stomach that night when Kevin recited his poetry on stage. She remembered the exact moment she fell in love with him, and it felt nice. Vince was beginning to awaken those same feelings inside her, and it scared her. She wasn't ready to feel this way again—about anyone.

Chapter 8

Vince sat casually at the bar, the ice in his Black Russian slowly melting away. It was his first drink all night. Light jazz filled the room as people were engaged in noisy conversations. Others slow-danced to the music. He kept his eye on the door and hoped she'd change her mind and show up. He needed to see her before he left the Bahamas, and he wanted to tell her that she'd stirred things in him that he'd never felt before. Sure, he'd dated many women in the past, had been in a few long-term relationships, but Sasha was the first woman to make his heart feel this way.

Bridget's friend Deja, who had been a thorn in his side the entire weekend, had managed to find her way over to him. He tried ignoring her at first, but she was a persistent one.

"Why are you sitting here all alone, boo, looking like you lost your best friend," she asked.

"Just enjoying the atmosphere. What about you?"

"Looking for you," she said enthusiastically. "Where have you been hiding all evening? I wanted my ride on that Jet Ski, too."

He looked at Deja. For the first time, he gave her a really good look. She had a pretty face, and a plus-size body. She would never be anyone he'd consider dating. Not because of her physical attributes, but because she was too forward, too clingy. He hated when women threw themselves at men and deprived them of the chase. He was a traditional man—and as such, he believed that men pursued women, not the other way around. She was a beautiful young woman, but her approach was all wrong.

"I wasn't hiding, Deja," he said.

"Are you supposed to be dating Sasha or something?"

"Not at the moment, but I'd like to get to know her." Vince was painfully honest. "Do you know Sasha very well?"

"Not all that well. She's Bridget's sister. A little stuck-up, in my opinion."

"Really?"

"Yeah, not much fun at all." Deja smiled and touched his knee. "Not like me…I'm lots of fun."

Vince grabbed Deja's hand and removed it from his knee. "You're such a beautiful woman. Why are you wasting your time chasing me around this resort?"

"Because you're fine as hell." She laughed at her own forwardness.

"You see that gentleman over there in the corner of the room?" Vince ignored her previous comment.

Deja started to turn her head to look.

"Don't look!" he said. "But he's been checking you out all night. Everywhere you move, his eyes move."

"Really?" she asked. "Can I look now?"

"Very slowly...turn around and look. Very subtly."

"Okay," she whispered, as if the man could hear her. She turned and found a Bahamian man seated at a table in a dark corner of the room. He was, in fact, looking their way.

The man raised his glass when Deja looked his way.

"Oh, my God! I think he *is* looking at me," said Deja, "and he is cute."

"Do not go near him. Don't even look his way again. I want you to act as if he's not even there," Vince ordered. "Give him the opportunity to come to you."

Deja gave Vince a nod. "Okay."

"This is what I want you to do," Vince said. "Go over and laugh with your girlfriends. Pretend to be having the time of your life. Totally ignore him. He'll find you."

"You think so?"

"Trust me on this."

Deja stood and sashayed over to the table where Bridget and her other girlfriends gathered. Vince watched as her bountiful behind wiggled across the room, and he shook his head. Her dress clung tightly to her body as she looked over her shoulder and gave Vince a quick smile. He gave her a nod encouraging her to continue. A few minutes later, the dapper Bahamian man approached Deja and asked her to dance. The couple moved to the center of the dance floor, and Vince smiled as he finished his drink. He took another glance at the door. He realized that Sasha wasn't coming, and that disappointed him.

He placed a twenty-dollar bill on the bar and bid everyone good-night. He strolled out into the beautiful night air and headed toward his condo. As he passed Sasha's room, he leaned with his back against the brick exterior wall for a moment. He contemplated knocking on her door but decided against it. She'd made her decision. If she wanted to let things be, whatever that meant, then he wouldn't fight her. He would respect her wishes.

He unlocked his door and tossed his door key on the coffee table. He pulled his suitcase out of the closet and placed it on top of the bed. He placed his Stacy Adams shoes into the suitcase first, carefully putting each into its own compartment. He was a fanatic about his shoes, and he was always carefully dressed. When he purchased a suit, he bought the tie, shirt and shoes all at the same time. He was practical about everything in his life except fashion. Fashion was his weakness. After packing each piece of clothing carefully into the suitcase, he took a long, hot shower and decided to turn in early.

Chapter 9

In her beachside condo, Sasha packed her things, show-ered and changed into pajamas. Her desire was to get some much-needed rest before heading home to At-lanta. The farewell cocktail party had not been high on her list of things to do. She'd had her fill of social gatherings for one weekend. In fact, as soon as she got back to Atlanta, it would be business as usual. She had a deposition that was awaiting her undivided attention.

The longer she sat there in front of the flat-screen television, the more those vivid thoughts of Vince crept into her mind. He'd managed to get under her skin after all. She thought of their encounter at the beach earlier and decided that things between them had been left undone, with no resolution or closure, and she felt as if there needed to be.

She hopped from the sofa and rushed to her closet in search of a dress. Something that would get his attention, something pretty, something red. She blow-dried her damp hair and styled it then slipped into the simple, sexy red dress and a pair of embellished sandals. After coloring her lips red and spraying on a few squirts of cologne, she grabbed her door key and headed for the cocktail party. She could hear the music before she reached the cabana, and when she stepped inside she headed for the bar.

"Sasha!" Bridget spotted her right away. "We're all over here. Why don't you join us?"

"I will. I just want to grab a drink first."

"I'll save you a seat."

Sasha stepped up to the bar and took a seat. She made a quick scan of the room, searching for Vince. When she didn't see him right away, she didn't go into a panic. She knew that he had a tendency of popping up unexpectedly. She smiled when she saw Deja dancing cheek to cheek with some Bahamian man. She had been determined to snag a man one way or the other while vacationing in the Bahamas, and it appeared as if she'd been successful. The music permeated in the room and provided the perfect ambiance. Sasha felt like dancing too. Where was her man when she needed him?

Her man. She toyed with the idea in her mind. She hadn't been open to it before, but she could see having a man like Vince in her life. Someone to talk to, or maybe catch a movie with from time to time. The idea of it wasn't all that far-fetched, she thought.

"What can I get you, ma'am?" asked the bartender.

"Just a house wine."

She scanned the room again—this time giving each corner a closer look. He wasn't there, and Sasha felt disappointed. It was his handsome face that had motivated her to step out of her comfortable space and get dressed in the middle of the night. And not seeing him there brought her down. She grabbed her drink and moseyed over to the corner of the room where her sister was seated and where the people around her were well ahead of her in inebriation. Bridget, who was sober, patted the chair next to her. Sasha took a seat.

"You look fabulous, big sis." Bridget gave her a hug, and whispered, "Is that a new dress?"

"This old thing?" Sasha said, and just as quickly hoped she'd remembered to snip the price tag off before leaving her condo.

Derrick smiled. "Glad you came out, Sasha. You just missed Vince. He said something about turning in early. He's got an early flight tomorrow. Just in case you were wondering."

Bridget interrupted. "She's not looking for Vince, silly. Why would she care about him turning in early?"

"I was just saying," said Derrick, "in case she wanted to know."

Sasha diverted her attention from the conversation and focused on her wine.

"Were you looking for Vince, Sasha?" Bridget asked.

"No, of course not. I came to celebrate with you and my new brother-in-law." She raised her glass to the newlyweds. "It's your last night in the Bahamas. A nice end to a beautiful weekend. I couldn't be happier for you two."

"Here, here," said Vanessa.

"Cheers!" said Taj, Derrick's groomsman who sat on the other side of him. "To a great weekend in the Bahamas."

Taj's wife raised her glass too. "We've had a fantastic time. It was just like a honeymoon for us too."

Taj and his wife shared a sensual kiss. Following suit, Bridget and Derrick shared one too. Sasha suddenly felt out of place. She wished Vince was there. It seemed that the two of them deserved a celebratory kiss, as well. After all, they'd already shared more than that. It had been an exciting weekend, yet Sasha had managed to allow it to end with her giving him the cold shoulder. She'd been rude and prudish, and a wave of guilt overcame her. If he walked through the door at that moment, she'd approach him—maybe ask him to dance. Perhaps they'd spend the evening snuggled in some corner of the room staring into each other's eyes. Maybe they'd exchange numbers and make plans to meet again in Atlanta.

As the evening progressed, the cocktail party became much more exuberant and Sasha found herself on the dance floor most of the night. She started out dancing in her seat, and a few drinks later she was on the floor doing the electric slide. It was a nice end to her vacation. Unfortunately, Vince didn't show up, and she found herself wondering when and if she'd ever see him again.

Chapter 10

Gabrielle Sullivan was a tall, model-like woman, with beautiful mocha skin and long, flowing hair. In heels, she stood almost as tall as Vince. When they were younger, she could easily beat him in a game of one-on-one or run just as fast up and down the block. In recent years, though, she'd outgrown her tomboyish manner, and it was difficult for Vince to come to terms with the change. He still saw her as his little sister, not the beautiful woman she had become.

She stood at the top of the escalator smiling and waving as he approached. With jeans that were too tight in Vince's opinion, a leather jacket and high-heeled boots, she could've easily graced the cover of any fashion magazine.

"You look all rested," Gabrielle said once he reached her.

"I feel well rested." Vince gave her a hug.

"Derrick was supposed to wait for me." She put on a pouty face. "I'd have married him in a heartbeat. I've always thought he was cute."

"Well, he's cute and married now. And way too old for you anyway."

"Not much older. And besides, women are dating older men these days, Vince," said Gabrielle. "I date older men these days."

"Not a subject I care to discuss, Gabby." Vince quickly moved toward baggage claim and Gabrielle followed.

"Why, Vincent? Why can't we discuss my love life? I'm just as grown as you are. And besides, I have someone I want you to meet."

"Who?"

"His name is Ronald."

"Does he know you have a crazy brother?"

"He knows you're a bit touched." Gabrielle laughed and Vince gave her a serious look. She sighed. "Yes, he knows that he must meet with your approval."

Vince waited for his bag to turn up on the carousel and once spotted, he grabbed it.

"Who is this guy anyway? And where did you meet him?"

"He's a stockbroker. And I met him through a mutual friend."

"Is he married?"

"No. Of course not."

"Any children or crazy baby mamas?"

"None of the above. He's single. No children. He has a master's in finance, owns a home and drives a nice car. He wears Hanes underwear. You know, the ones that are endorsed by Michael Jordan?"

"Ha-ha, very funny, little girl." Vince squeezed her nose as he used to when she was a young girl.

"See, that's just it, Vince. I'm not a little girl anymore. And you have to stop treating me like one."

"When you're ninety-two years old, you'll still be my little sister."

"That's if you're still alive when I'm ninety-two."

"Even if I'm dead and gone, you'll still be my little sister. And I'll still need to approve of that old geezer that you've met in the nursing home—you know the one that'll be gumming his soup because he can't find his false teeth. I'll come back and haunt you both."

"You are so stupid." Gabrielle laughed heartily and so did Vince.

Vince grabbed Gabrielle by the neck, pulled her close and planted a kiss on her forehead. "But you love me though."

"I do love you," she said. "And I missed your peanut head, too."

"You up for a game of basketball tomorrow after your classes?"

"Nah. I'm meeting Ronald for lunch in Midtown and probably a matinee at the movies."

"Are you kidding me? Now you're blowing me off for this Ronald dude?" Vince looked wounded. "Unbelievable!"

"I'm not blowing you off. But I do have a life, Vincent." Gabrielle smiled. "You should get you one too. Find you a nice woman and settle down. When you gonna do that?"

"We're not talking about my life. We're talking about yours."

"Maybe we should talk about your life. Didn't you meet anyone in the Bahamas?"

Vince was silent.

"Oh, my God, you met someone in the Bahamas! Who?"

"No one really."

"You're such a liar!"

"Nobody special. Just some woman I'll probably never see again. End of story."

"Does she live in the Bahamas? Is she one of those island girls with a beautiful accent?"

"She lives in Atlanta."

"Seriously? Then why won't you see her again? I don't understand."

"I don't think she's interested."

"You like her," Gabrielle stated matter-of-factly. "You should see your face when you talk about her! You're trying to be all hard, but I see right through that."

Vince tried to maintain a poker face for his sister, but it wasn't working. He smiled a little. He did like Sasha. He liked her more than she or anyone else knew.

"When can I meet her?" she asked.

"I just said she's not interested. I really don't think she wants to see me again. So the quick answer is... never."

"Why wouldn't she want to see you again?" Gabrielle gave Vince an inquisitive look. "What did you do to her?"

"I didn't do anything...except..."

"Except what?"

"I didn't do anything to her. She's just not interested, okay?"

"When has that ever stopped you? You always go after what you want."

She was correct. Vince usually did go after what he

wanted, and he was usually pretty successful at getting it.

"Not this time," he said. He would go on with life as he knew it. What he shared with Sasha had been short-lived. He had his memories, and that would have to suffice.

He tossed his bag into the trunk of Gabrielle's BMW and hopped into the passenger's seat, snapped on his seat belt and placed a pair of dark sunglasses on his face. As she breezed down Interstate 285, Vince rested his head against the leather seat and shut his eyes. He hoped that Sasha Winters would not creep into his dreams again.

Chapter 11

The smell of fried chicken and collard greens hit Vince's nose the minute he walked into the house. Leaving his suitcase at the front door, he made a beeline for the kitchen. A mountain of golden-brown chicken rested on a platter. He found collard greens, mashed potatoes and a cast-iron skillet filled with corn bread on the stove. There was no doubt, his mother had been there and prepared dinner for him.

Dolores Sullivan was a thoughtful woman, and she loved her children. She was an older, more beautiful version of Gabrielle—tall and dark with just a hint of gray in her hair. She had a plump figure that had probably been considered pleasantly plump in her day. She was a widow who had single-handedly raised two children by herself. She'd moved her family from New Jersey to Atlanta when Vince was in elementary school, with hopes of providing a better life. The cost of living was better for sure, and the schools were much safer for Vince and Gabrielle. She had worked two jobs—sometimes three just to make ends meet—and was determined to put both of her children through college. To Vince, she was the greatest woman in the world.

Years after Vince's father passed away, Dolores discovered trust funds that he'd established for his children the very day he died. The trusts had earned an enormous amount of interest over the years and were worth millions of dollars by the time Vince and his sister became young adults. Vince had bought a house and a car with his, as well as paid off his mother's mortgage and his student loans. He'd invested the rest.

He grabbed a chicken leg and took a bite before taking the stairs to his master bedroom. His laundry had been done also and put away in its rightful place. It wasn't unusual for his mother to spend the weekend at his east Atlanta home, especially when he wasn't there. Whenever she visited, she always made it a point to prepare a nice meal for him and to do his laundry. When in college, he would often drop his laundry off at home for his mother. Things hadn't changed much—instead of him dropping his clothes off, she came to his house.

He dialed her number and she picked up on the second ring.

"The chicken is fire," he said.

"I guess that means it's good." Dolores had a smile in her voice.

"That means it's really good. You're too much, Ma. Cooking for me and doing my laundry. That's why I love you."

"You love me because I do your laundry?"

"No, because you take such great care of me."

"It's my pleasure to take care of you, sweetie," said

Dolores. "Glad to see that you're back safe and sound. Was Gabby on time to pick you up?"

"Yeah, she was. She just dropped me off. She was dressed in these tight jeans and high-heeled boots. Did you see her before she left the house?"

"She has her own place now, Vincent. Remember?"

"Oh, yeah. I try to forget about that little piece of real estate that she purchased last month. I probably need to take a look at her portfolio and see how she's spending her money."

"She's a grown-up, honey. A big girl."

"I know. I just don't want her spending carelessly. And I don't want anyone using her for her money either. Did she tell you about what's-his-name?"

"Oh, you mean Ronald?"

"You met him?"

"He's a nice young man, Vince. I think you'll like him. Just as mannerly as he wants to be, and he's got a good job—" she paused, waited for a reaction from Vince "—and he's a nice-looking fellow."

"Can't wait to meet him so I can give him the third degree."

"Don't be too hard on him, Vincent. She really likes him." Dolores changed the subject. "So how was the wedding? I want to hear all about it. I bet Derrick looked as handsome as ever! And his bride was probably drop-dead gorgeous."

"The wedding was very nice, Ma." Vince placed his mother on speakerphone while he changed into a pair of sweats and his New York Giants jersey. "As a matter of fact, Derrick will be here in a minute. We're watching the game."

"Isn't he still on his honeymoon? Has he already

abandoned that new wife of his for Monday night football?"

"It's what we do, Ma. Bridget knows that. That's not going to stop because he got married."

"I guess not. I'm glad I fried enough chicken."

"Oh, I'm not sharing my chicken!" Vince had already made plans to wrap the chicken in foil and stick it in the oven. "Taj and Mike are coming too. And I'm not sharing with them either. This is a BYOMF...bring your own mama's food."

Dolores laughed heartily. "You are some kind of mess, boy. I didn't teach you to be selfish. You share that chicken with your friends."

The doorbell rang and Vince knew it was probably one of them.

"Gotta go, Ma. One of them knuckleheads is here."

"Okay, baby. Have a good time." Dolores understood Vince's love for football. She had been a sports mom for a long time. She'd spent many a day cheering in the stands at his games, transporting him and his friends to practices, working the concession stands and helping with fundraisers.

"I will."

After hanging up, he rushed down the stairs and swung the door open.

"I brought the Heineken." Derrick raised a six-pack of beer into the air, shook hands with Vince and stepped inside. He headed for the kitchen. "Wait a minute. Is that Mama Sullivan's fried chicken I smell?"

"No...no, it's not." Vince followed his friend.

Derrick spotted the chicken with a wide grin on his face. Vince stood in front of the stove with his arms stretched wide.

"Come on, man. Why you being so stingy?"

The doorbell rang and interrupted him. He warned Derrick, "Don't touch anything! I'll be right back."

The minute Vince left the kitchen Derrick grabbed a crisp piece of chicken and bit into it. He closed his eyes and savored the taste. He knew that flavor quite well. He'd spent many days at the Sullivan household growing up and ate many meals there. Dolores Sullivan was a second mother to him, and she'd fed him often. He took another bite and yelled from the kitchen, "This is good, V!"

Vince greeted Taj and Mike at the door.

"Hey, what's up, bro?" said Taj and shook Vince's hand. "What time is kickoff?"

"Five minutes," said Vince.

"We're just in time. I tried to get here sooner, but Pretty Boy Floyd here was too busy primping as if there were some women over here."

"I have to look good before I leave the house," said Mike. "You never know who or what you might run into."

Vince took Mike's hand in a firm handshake. "And you're still as ugly as ever. So I don't understand."

Vince and Taj laughed. Mike didn't.

"You ready to see those Giants get spanked tonight? That's what you should understand." Mike carried a case of Coke underneath his arm. "I see you're wearing your tired, faded L.T. jersey."

Vince had been a diehard Giants fan for years. Even after his family moved to Atlanta, he remained a fan of New York since elementary school. Lawrence Taylor had long been his favorite player in the league, and he'd worn the same jersey since college. "I think you already know whose game this is, right?"

The Giants were playing their rival team, which happened to be Mike's team of choice. He wore a blue Cowboys jersey with a long-sleeved turtleneck underneath. "Yeah, I do know whose game it is. Cowboys, of course."

"Is that fried chicken I smell?" Taj interrupted their banter. He knew the answer to his question when he saw Derrick at the dining room table with a plate filled with chicken, greens and mashed potatoes.

"Your mother's been here," Mike said matter-of-factly.

"What makes you think that, man? I know how to cook," said Vince. "I don't need my mother to cook for me."

"He *can* cook," Taj agreed with Vince.

Taj was the most amenable person Vince knew. He'd never been into it with Taj. There was no reason to. Taj had never been a confrontational person. On the contrary, he was an expert at defusing hostile situations. Taj had married his high school sweetheart, Elaine, and the couple had lived in the city of Atlanta since college. He was the poster child for the American dream—beautiful wife, beautiful house, two cars, two children and church on Sunday. At least it appeared that way.

"That may be true. Nobody's debating his cooking skills. In fact, his cooking skills are a lot better than his football skills." Mike laughed at his own criticism of Vince.

Mike was the competitive one. He was great at diminishing someone else's light so that his could shine brighter. If someone bought a car, he needed a faster one. If someone met a new woman, he needed a prettier one. It was his nature. "I know your mother's fried chicken. I've eaten it enough over the years to recognize it by smell."

Mike had been the quarterback for their college team, and he had been the star of the squad. Unfortunately, he hadn't quite made the transition from being a star in college to becoming a star in real life. He thought that he was supposed to receive the same free ride in life that he'd received in college. By the time the reality of it hit him it was too late. He'd wasted too much time drinking and partying while life-changing opportunities had passed him by. He'd become an insurance agent instead of the engineer that he'd gone to school to become, and the fact of it haunted him daily. Consequently, he wasn't pleased with himself or his career and had turned to drinking as a coping mechanism. After a serious drunken driving incident and several AA meetings later, he was a recovering alcoholic.

"He's right about that," Derrick yelled from the dining table, his mouth full. "Your mother's food does have a distinct smell."

"Gimme the Coke, man." Vince grabbed the soda from Mike's arms and took it to the kitchen.

Mike followed, got a plate off the shelf and didn't hesitate to load it with food. "Did she make dessert too?"

Vince gave him a cross-eyed look.

The four of them had been friends as far back as Vince could remember. He'd met Derrick in ninth grade and Taj in the eleventh grade. Mike had joined the trio their freshmen year at Georgia State when the four of them played football together. Of the three, Vince had been closest with Derrick.

Derrick was a genuine person and a man of his word. He did what he said he would do. Sometimes in life, adjustments were warranted. Derrick didn't handle adjustments very well. There was no deviating from his plan, which is why his engagement to Bridget was a rocky one. The guest list had changed a dozen times, and the venue twice. And finally, the wedding date had been pushed up three times. Vince thought Derrick would abandon the plans altogether.

When Derrick first met Bridget, Vince wondered if the pair would last three months. They were as different as night and day. Bridget was extravagant; Derrick was prudent. Bridget could be flighty; Derrick was sensible. However, their love had withstood the test of time. Derrick had become more accommodating.

"Seriously, bro," Derrick mumbled, "I would get a plate quickly if I were you. I'm just about ready for seconds myself."

"Hey, Vince, I saw you being kind of clingy with that broad over the weekend. You know, Derrick's sister-in-law. What was up with that?" Mike usually just came right out and asked whatever it was he wanted to know. His style was intrusive and usually rude. Mike was Vince's friend who couldn't seem to settle down; he didn't think any woman was worthy of him. In Vince's opinion, he couldn't settle down because he couldn't seem to get past his own self-hatred.

"Not that it's any of your business…we were just having a conversation."

"Sasha's cool," Derrick added. "She's really into her career, but she's a decent person."

"I think she's beautiful," said Taj. "And I think while we're on the subject, V, you should start thinking about settling down. Find yourself a good woman and have some kids. That's what it's all about."

"That's not what it's all about," Mike argued. "Once you settle down with a woman, your life is over. You no longer have control of your life. Suddenly you got somebody in your ear every day of your life, nagging...and nagging. I'm never settling. Too many fish in the sea."

"I made the plunge," Derrick said. "It took me a minute because I had all these goals that I wanted to achieve beforehand. But that went out the window. The reality of it is, when you find the right woman, and you know it...then you have to follow your heart."

"Yeah, she definitely had your nose wide open," Mike said to Derrick. "That's why you were married a month earlier than planned. And you'll probably be a daddy before the year is over. Watch what I tell you."

"Derrick is right," Taj agreed. "When you find the right woman, you follow your heart."

Mike shook his head. "And this from a man who married his high school sweetheart. You never had the opportunity to stray a little, so how would you know if she's the right woman? You never even had any strange booty."

"I've had strange booty," said Taj.

The men laughed heartily at Taj's rebuttal. Mike had a way of making a fool of Taj, and once again, he'd fallen right into the trap.

"Who have you had sex with since high school besides Elaine?" Mike asked.

Taj was silent. Vince was the only one who knew that it had been less than a year since Taj had an affair. He'd caught Elaine cheating, and as a result he'd had a fling of his own. After ending the affair and confessing it to his wife, Taj and Elaine vowed to never cheat on each other again. They were working on their marriage.

Vince rescued Taj from the discomfort of Mike's ranting. "I say we go downstairs and watch those Cowgirls get spanked by the Giants."

"Yeah let's," said Mike. "The Giants don't have a

chance in hell of beating the Cowboys. You know it, I know it and the Giants know it."

The two men argued all the way down to the basement. With all the talk of women and marriage and settling down, Vince thought of Sasha. He wondered if she was the woman he was supposed to have a future with. He wondered if he even wanted a future with anyone. Taj's marital issues had caused him to be gunshy; they'd made him afraid of marriage. That was before bumping into Sasha, though. After spending time with her, he could actually see himself settling down for the first time. If she'd just let go of her inhibitions, she might be able to see it too.

Chapter 12

Sasha stepped into her office and placed her briefcase on the corner of Keira's desk.

"Good morning."

"Got your Frappuccino," said Keira, handing Sasha her drink and a stack of messages. "Glad to see you back."

"Glad to be back," Sasha said and flipped through her messages. "What's the mood like around here?"

"Quiet, for now. But give it time. Kirby will be up to her usual tricks soon. Everyone understood about your being stuck in Nassau. Except Kyle of course." Keira lowered her voice. "He's asinine. "But other than being stranded, how was your trip?"

"It was very nice. And being stranded wasn't so bad."

"Really? That can only mean one thing…you were stranded with a man!"

"How does that mean that?"

"I know you, Sasha Winters. You would not be happy about being stranded and missing that retreat. That was too important to miss. No, there's something more to this story."

"What are you talking about?"

"Your face is different." Keira gave her a closer look. "You look like you got your groove back! Just like Terry McMillan did in *Waiting to Exhale*."

Keira was an avid reader and had an active imagination. Sasha often accused her of living vicariously through the books that she read. Sometimes she had trouble separating the stories from real life.

"And what does that look like, Keira? What does it mean to get your groove back?"

"It means you're glowing."

"You're crazy."

"Am I? Sasha Winters, you met a man," Keira insisted. "Now, tell me you didn't."

"Okay, I did." Sasha smiled and then hushed Keira. "But keep your voice down."

"I want all the details, Sasha, and I mean it." Keira smiled. "But first, Kyle's waiting in your office. He wants to see you."

"About what?" Sasha frowned.

"Who knows? But you and I will talk later about this new man."

Sasha wouldn't be boasting about a new man at all. Vince had turned out to be just like all the other men in the world—predictable. Just when she'd come to terms with her feelings about him, she'd spotted him at Harts-field-Jackson International Airport with a gorgeous woman. He'd wrapped his arms around her; kissed her. Sasha had fought the urge to confront him. She'd had a good mind to walk right up to them at baggage claim and let this woman know exactly what he'd been up to while away in the Bahamas.

Before reaching Atlanta, thoughts of Vince had her giddy. She'd found herself thinking of him during the entire flight and wondering what he was doing, whether or not he'd made it home safely or whether he was thinking of her. However, after seeing him with that woman at the airport, she'd attempted to erase all memories of him. Every intimate moment had been a lie and didn't deserve another minute of her time, she thought. She wouldn't allow him to absorb her thoughts or energy. Her plan was to bury herself in work, just as she always had. It was what she was accustomed to.

Kyle was seated in the brown leather chair in the corner of Sasha's office. With legs crossed, he spoke firmly with someone on his cell phone. When he saw Sasha, he held up his index finger in order to indicate "one minute" as if he were in his own office. Sasha resented his arrogance, but she endured it.

After Kyle ended his call, he looked at Sasha, "And what exactly was it that had you detained over the weekend?"

"I was stuck in the Bahamas due to a terrible storm. It was beyond my control." Sasha pulled a manila file from her briefcase and then sat at her desk. "The phone lines were down. But once I was able to use my phone, I asked Keira to inform you."

"I got the message, Sasha, but missing the retreat wasn't a good move for you. You're at a very critical time in your career, and not showing up for such an important event…I mean…"

"It couldn't be helped, Kyle," explained Sasha.

Secretly she was happy that she'd missed the retreat. The time she'd spent in the Bahamas had been far more entertaining than rubbing elbows with snobbish people from the industry. She felt guilty for feeling that way, but she couldn't help it. The trip had done her a world of good; revived her. Even if things hadn't worked out with Vince, she was a new woman, with a new outlook on life.

Sometime during the conversation with Kyle, she'd checked out.

"Is that good for you?" he was asking.

"Is what good for me?"

"A staff meeting this afternoon at three. I'd like to go over our caseload and figure out which cases are better suited for Kirby, and which ones are a better fit for you."

"Sure, Kyle. No problem."

A light tap on the door interrupted their conversation.

"Sorry to interrupt, Sasha, but these just arrived for you." Keira walked into Sasha's office carrying a vase filled with a dozen coral roses. "It's got a card too," she pointed out with a smile. Keira placed the vase on Sasha's desk.

"Thank you, Keira," said Sasha.

"Hmm…a secret admirer?" Kyle asked.

"Not sure." Sasha grabbed the card and slipped it into the pocket of her slacks without opening it.

"They're coral," explained Keira with a smile. "Coral roses convey desire."

"Thank you, Keira. That will be all," Sasha insisted, and Keira winked as she exited the office.

"Who are they from?" Kyle asked, inappropriately.

Kyle was a handsome man. Shorter than average height, he looked like a younger version of his older brother, Louis. He wore tailored suits and perfectly shined shoes. His hair was always freshly cut, and he wore a precisely trimmed goatee. Kyle always smelled of the latest, most expensive fragrances.

She'd always liked Louis and had a great deal of respect for him, but not so much for Kyle. Johnson, Johnson and Donovan was one of the oldest firms in the Atlanta area. Established by their father, Gregory Johnson, in the early sixties, it was known for its strong ethics and respect for the law. Greg Johnson built his firm on fairness and hired only the best attorneys. Louis tried hard to maintain the standards set by their father. However, Sasha wasn't sure that Kyle shared their father's values. And she knew that Kirby Alexander sure didn't. Her intentions were to make a name for herself, not to expand the company. Sasha had a great deal of respect for the Johnson family and knew that the firm was in trouble with Louis retiring. She knew that the best way to maintain the integrity of the firm would be for them to make her partner. She had the knowledge and experience, but most of all she had the heart for it.

Ignoring his question, she said, "Yes, Kyle. Three o'clock works just fine for me. I'll see you then?"

With a surprised look on his face, Kyle stood and walked over to the door. He'd been dismissed and didn't know how to respond. "I'll see you at three." He lingered near the door for a moment and then walked out, but not soon enough.

Once he was gone, Sasha closed the door. She was anxious to get to the card that accompanied the breathtaking bouquet. She pulled it out of her pocket and opened it. It read: *Enjoyed every second with you. I know you said to let it be, but I can't get you out of my head. Have dinner with me tonight...Starbucks, 14th Street & Peachtree, 6pm. P.S. Wear jeans. Vince.*

"Wear jeans?" Sasha whispered to herself. "And since when did Starbucks serve dinner?"

A knock at the door interrupted her thoughts, and the door opened quickly. Keira slipped in like a cat burglar and eased the door shut behind her. She took a seat on the leather love seat in Sasha's office and crossed her legs.

"Now! Who is this man that is expressing desire for you with coral roses?"

"His name is Vince. He was the best man at Bridget and Derrick's wedding. We sort of...hit it off."

"Sort of hit it off, Sasha?" Keira asked. "What does that mean?"

"Okay, we hit it off pretty well."

"Is he cute? Never mind. That was a dumb question. Of course he is."

"Very handsome. Tall and dark with the cutest dimples." Sasha giggled.

"Is he married or have children?"

"I'm not sure. I saw him being picked up at the airport by some woman. They were quite cozy. It was probably his wife or a girlfriend."

"Could've been a friend, or his sister or a distant cousin even."

"He kissed her," said Sasha.

"On the mouth?"

"No...the forehead, but still..."

"Don't assume things, Sasha. Ask him about her. These roses don't say...I'm married or in a relationship. They say I'm very interested in you! Men don't send bouquets like this for nothing. These were carefully chosen."

"That might be true."

"So…where is this thing going? You dating him? You planning on giving up the booty?"

Sasha looked sheepish.

"What's that look?" Keira covered her mouth. "Oh, my God, Sasha Winters! You already gave up the booty?"

"Shh! Keep your voice down." Sasha smiled. "When you say it like that, it makes it sound so cheap."

"Sorry."

"Besides, you told me to have a good time."

"That I did," Keira said with a laugh. "I didn't tell you to give up the booty, but I guess if it was good… then…I'm happy for you, Sasha. You deserve love and happiness."

"Not so fast. He might be hitched."

"Or not."

"Or not," Sasha agreed, a glimmer of hope in her voice. It was worth finding out who the woman was before she jumped to conclusions. She sighed. "Thanks, Keira. Now, I'm not trying to put you out, but I really have a lot of work to catch up on."

"Fine. I'm leaving," Keira stood, "but before I go, please tell me you're going to see him again."

"I might." Sasha blushed. The truth was she'd already calculated the number of hours before she met him at Starbucks.

Keira took one last smell of the roses. "He's got good taste."

Sasha nodded a yes. He did have good taste, she thought.

Everyone had already taken their usual seats around the conference table by the time Sasha entered the room. Taking her place next to Louis, she opened her iPad and searched for her list of cases. Kyle opened the meeting by bragging about the retreat and how worthwhile it had been for all who attended—making sure he glanced at Sasha when emphasizing the words *all who attended*.

"Louis has been handling our biggest client, the Pro-Tek Pharmaceutical account. However, as we all know, Louis has one foot out the door and will be pursuing a career on the golf course soon. We need someone who is fully capable of taking over the representation of this client," said Kyle. "Of course, I think that Kirby would work best…"

Louis interrupted. "Excuse me, Kyle. Don't mean to interrupt, but I think that Sasha would be better at representing ProTek. She has more experience, and she's assisted me on this account in the past. This company has very complex legal affairs, and I think that Sasha is fully capable of handling them."

Sasha gave Louis a warm smile. The Louis she remembered was back. He'd always protected her in the past.

"They're currently in litigation against one of their employees," Kyle reminded the staff. "We need someone who is shrewd."

"I'm familiar with the owners of the company, and I'm sure that Louis can quickly bring me up to speed on the details of the case." Sasha wanted this case. It was a great way to move closer to her goal. "I can do this, Kyle."

"No offense, Sasha," Kirby chimed in, "but you're not as shrewd as I am…"

"No offense taken, Kirby," Sasha stated, "and you're absolutely correct…I'm not as shrewd as you are. I don't think anyone is. However, I am a more seasoned attorney, I'm familiar with ProTek and I'm a barracuda in the courtroom."

"ProTek is an important client, Sasha," said Kyle.

"I'm aware of that."

"You would have to devote most of your time to this one," explained Kyle, "and you'd have to be careful not to let your personal life interfere."

"We all have personal lives, Kyle. And for the record, I've never allowed my personal life to interfere with my professional life."

"It would require your undivided attention."

"For crying out loud, Kyle. She's just taking on a case, not performing heart surgery," said Louis.

"Don't disappoint us," Kyle finally said.

Sasha smiled inside. It felt good to be depended on— to be trusted to handle such an important client. She knew that representing ProTek could easily launch her into the partner position that she'd had her sights on for so long. She knew the background on the company. ProTek's business practices were somewhat questionable, but someone had to represent it. Even though many consumers are harmed by drugs because pharmaceutical companies fail to warn them about certain risks, Sasha knew that it was simply the nature of the beast. As an attorney it was her job to protect her client, and if it got her the corner office with a view, she'd learn to live with it.

"I won't disappoint, Kyle."

"This can't take a backseat to your personal life," Kyle reiterated.

"Johnson, Johnson and Donovan *is* my life," said Sasha.

Sasha was engaged in a war, and obtaining the ProTek account was one step closer to winning a battle.

The look of defeat on Kirby's face was priceless. Sasha knew that Kyle would have to pay for this for weeks to come. She left the meeting feeling a sense of victory that she hadn't felt in a long time.

Chapter 13

Starbucks was crowded and loud conversations over-powered the light coffeehouse music. People were scat-tered about—some of them pecking on the keys of their laptops, while others were engaged in quiet conversa-tions. Sasha had chosen the best-fitting pair of jeans in her closet and a nice colorful top—the one that brought out the brown in her skin. She'd applied a natural-col-ored eye shadow with matching lip gloss, and had traced her eyes with black eyeliner. She'd sprayed a few squirts of perfume, but not too much.

Just enough to entice without being abrasive.

She searched for Vince but didn't see him right away. Her instructions were to meet him at Starbucks, but that was all she had to go on. He'd extended an invitation for dinner, but Starbucks was far from a restaurant and she wondered what Vince had up his sleeve. When she saw him stroll through the door, it felt as if her breath had left her. His presence had a profound effect on her. She pretended not to be moved, but it was hard.

She loved his handsome face, and she instantly reflected on the night they'd made love to each other. The thought of it made her toes tingle. She'd gone over it a million times in her mind—tried to erase the memory, but it was useless. She couldn't help reliving every moment of it. Wanted to make sense of it. Casual sex had never been her style. She'd always been in a committed relationship long before lovemaking had come into play. But something caused her to be relaxed enough with this man to allow him in places that were normally off-limits.

Vince caught her eye and then moved quickly in her direction.

He gave her a strong hug and then kissed her cheek. "Hi, you. I couldn't wait to see your beautiful face again."

"Hello." She gave him a warm smile but remained standoffish.

Before she would let her guard down, she needed answers to a few questions.

"How long have you been waiting?" he asked.

A lifetime for someone to make me feel alive again— the way I feel with you, she wanted to say. But instead she said, "Not long. Just walked in."

"What are you drinking?" Vince asked before approaching the counter.

Sasha shrugged. "I don't know. I've already had my daily Frappuccino, so maybe a latte. Vanilla."

"Cool," said Vince and then ordered Sasha an iced vanilla latte and a Caramel Skinny Macchiato for himself.

He managed to snag a small corner table where the

two of them sipped their drinks and talked about everything under the sun. It seemed as if they were the only two people in the room, and an hour had passed before she got around to asking him about the woman at the airport.

"I saw you at the airport with a woman the other day. Now, I know that we're not dating or in any type of committed relationship or anything like that, but I don't mess around with other people's men. So if you're married or have a girlfriend…"

Vince interrupted. "I'm not married, and I don't have a girlfriend. The woman you saw me with at the airport was Gabby, my sister."

Sasha felt embarrassed yet relieved all at the same time. She exhaled. "I'm sorry. I just thought…"

"You were jealous." Vince grinned.

"I wasn't jealous," Sasha lied.

"Not even a little bit?"

"Okay, maybe a little."

"You were somewhere in that airport stalking me?" Vince laughed heartily.

"I wasn't stalking you. I just observed you from a distance."

"Why didn't you just come over and say hello? I would've introduced you."

Sasha admitted, "I wasn't quite in that frame of mind. When I saw you with that woman, I wanted to forget about you."

"And now?"

"And now, I guess I don't."

"You guess? You're not certain?"

"Okay, I don't want to forget about you."

"I'm very glad you had a change of heart." Vince

checked his watch and then stood. "We have to go or we'll be late."

"Late for what?"

"Our reservations," he simply said.

Sasha followed Vince through the crowded café and out the door.

Once in the parking lot, Vince said, "Leave your car. You can ride with me."

"I don't know. I don't ride in cars with strange men."

"Are you serious?" Vince stood there in awe.

"Very. I don't know anything about you—where you live…"

"I live in Stone Mountain, Georgia. What else?"

"I don't have your phone number, don't know your mother's name or where you work." Sasha folded her arms across her chest.

"You're being ridiculous." Vince pulled his phone out of his pocket and dialed a number. "Hey, Ma. It's me. Look, I need a favor. I'm going to hand this young woman my phone. I want you to explain to her who I am and that she can feel safe going on a date with me. Yes, ma'am. Her name is Sasha. No, ma'am. Okay, I'm going to hand her the phone."

Sasha mouthed, "What are you doing?"

Before she could say another word, Vince held the phone out to her. She took it reluctantly. "Hello?"

"Hello, this is Dolores Sullivan. I'm Vincent's mother. And you are?"

"I'm Sasha Winters."

"Nice to meet you, Sasha. If you haven't already figured it out, my son is very canny and very persistent. He's probably different from anyone you've ever met."

"Yes, ma'am, he is," Sasha agreed.

"I often tell him that he missed his calling. He

should've been a salesman." Dolores chuckled. "But then on the other hand, he has a big heart, so he fits very well with the career that he's chosen. Are you the young lady he met in the Bahamas?"

"Yes, I am."

"He really likes you. I've never seen him make a fuss over a woman before. Calling me on the phone… interrupting my show, *Dancing with the Stars*. Is it just me, or is Gladys Knight looking younger these days?"

Sasha was speechless.

"Anyway, I know you don't want to hear about Gladys Knight. You want to know if my son is a good man or not. Well, I know that he has his flaws. He's got some control issues, but overall he's decent…"

Vince's mother went on and on about her son. Sasha couldn't understand why, but after speaking with her, she felt more comfortable riding with Vince. What man actually puts his mother on the phone? After Sasha was done talking with Dolores Sullivan, she handed Vince his phone back.

He strolled over to the black convertible sports car, hit the locks and held the passenger door open.

"This is your car? I never thought you to be a Corvette guy."

"I'm really very practical. In fact, I rarely bring her out—only for special occasions like this," Vince said.

"I see," Sasha said and then slid comfortably into the bucket seat. She quickly fastened her seat belt.

As he whipped the car out of the Starbucks parking lot, she knew that there was more to Vince than met the eye. With a quick press of a button, Jay-Z's voice rang through the speakers.

"If you want to hear something different, we can change it."

Although rap wasn't really her style of music, she didn't protest. She was simply enjoying this side of Vince that she hadn't known existed. He was dressed in stylish jeans and a gray cashmere sweater, with gray Jordan sneakers. His outfit was not one that she'd expected to see him wearing, but she liked it.

"It's okay. I can get down with some Jay-Z occasionally," she said and smiled.

"That's good, because you might hear any type of music while hanging out with me—everything from hardcore rap to Beethoven. I like it all. I'm a music fanatic!"

"I like music too, but I'm sort of loyal to a few select genres and artists."

"That's cool, but you'd be surprised what you might like if you branched out a little."

Vince zoomed down Peachtree Street toward downtown Atlanta. Downtown was lit up as usual with its bright lights and bumper-to-bumper traffic. The skyline was as beautiful as the autumn night. As they approached Philips Arena, Sasha took in the crowds that stood in long lines outside waiting to enter the building. It was always crowded on a night when an NBA basketball game took place. Before Sasha knew it, Vince had pulled into the parking garage at the arena and shut off the car's engine.

"Hawks are playing the Heat tonight. Best game of the season and we have club seats."

Vince grinned.

Sasha frowned. Basketball? Hadn't he invited her to dinner? She wasn't the least bit interested in seeing grown men running up and down a basketball court. Not to mention her stomach was growling because she'd passed on lunch in an effort to preserve her appetite for dinner.

Sasha sat there for a moment. She was confused.

"Trust me," Vince said after noticing her hesitation. "I promise you won't be disappointed."

Trust him? It had been a long time since she'd trusted a man. And the last time she'd done so, it ended badly. She'd lost sight of her own values and had missed all the red flags and found herself hurt. Trust was something that had to be earned. Her mind knew this, but her heart was already wearing down.

She unsnapped her seat belt and reluctantly stepped out of the car. Vince rushed around to the passenger side of the car, grabbed Sasha's hand and intertwined his fingers with hers while the two of them made their way into the arena. The walk was longer than Sasha anticipated. Although Vince had asked her to wear jeans, she'd decided to dress them up with four-inch heels. She hadn't expected to do much walking—after all, most Atlanta restaurants offered valet parking, so the most walking she thought she'd be doing would be from the car to the door of the restaurant. Her goal for the night had simply been to look cute and become reacquainted with the man who'd stolen her heart in the Bahamas.

She certainly wasn't in the mood for hot dogs and nachos from one of the vendors in the arena, and she hoped that wasn't what Vince had in mind either. As they drifted through the arena, Vince was engaged in brief conversations with several people—many who knew him by name. He offered high fives to youngsters whom he recognized and warm hugs and firm handshakes to older people. It was quite clear that he was no stranger in this place, and it seemed that everyone knew him. He introduced Sasha as his good friend to those who lingered for an introduction.

"But I'm working on making her much more than that," he explained to one older gentleman in particular.

"I can see why," the older man said with a grin. "She's beautiful."

"She's the attorney I was telling you about, Otis," said Vince. "I'll see if I can pick her brain for you."

"Do that, man," Otis said. "I really could use some help."

"You holding up all right otherwise?" Vince asked.

"About as well as can be expected."

"Taja missed our last two practices. Is everything all right?"

"It's just been tough getting her there. But I promise she won't miss another one."

"Good! And bring her in to see me about those teeth too," Vince said.

"You know I lost my job. I don't have my dental plan anymore. In fact, I don't have health care or any benefits anymore. It's a tough world when you're out of work."

"Bring her in to see me anyway," Vince insisted.

When Otis shook Vince's hand again, he held on to it this time. There was a moment of friendship shared between the two men, and it warmed Sasha's heart. She gave Otis a smile. He seemed like a sincere man, and she wondered about his plight—why he was suffering, and why Vince had opened his heart to him. She didn't understand why, but it made Vince that much more interesting. She loved the many facets of him and couldn't wait to discover the rest. Even though she wasn't quite settled with Vince's idea of a date, she was feeling a little better about the evening.

They took the escalator to the upper level of Philips Arena. They strolled past the food court, and Sasha wondered which vendor would be providing their feast for the evening. She was confused when Vince passed up the food court but was pleasantly surprised when they entered a sleek restaurant with red, black and gray decor. Red, written in bold red letters, with a martini glass in the center of the letter *D,* was the name of the upscale, yet casual restaurant inside Philips Arena. The restaurant boasted a premium view of the action on the floor. Vince had thoughtfully reserved a small table on the terrace, where they could enjoy a nice, elegant dinner and still take in every moment of the Hawks game.

Sasha had never been much of a sports fan, but as Vince began to explain every play on the court, she suddenly found herself engaged. When he rooted for the Hawks, she cheered them on, as well. When he admonished a player for making a foolish play, she offered her own reprimand. She began to see basketball in a new light. And enjoying it with Vince made it seem so much better. By the end of the night, she knew who Josh Smith was and knew why Lebron James's nickname was "King James." She felt as if she'd been accepted into an exclusive club, and she loved it.

After dinner, Vince escorted Sasha to their box seats, where they continued watching the game. They talked during the downtimes, and Sasha learned a little bit more about the man who was slowly easing into her heart. He was interesting and charming, and she tried to imagine her life before he had waltzed into it. Had he not rescued her that very evening, she'd have been at home in front of her laptop computer, or she'd have her nose stuck inside a law book. And neither of those things could hold a candle to the evening she was having.

The drive back to Starbucks seemed shorter than the

earlier drive to Philips Arena. She knew that there was some truth to the saying that time flew when you were having fun. And she was definitely having fun. On the drive back, Vince had slowed the music down to a much more romantic taste than Jay-Z's rhythmic chatter. As Will Downing's rich baritone filled the Corvette, Sasha found herself slouching in the passenger seat. She'd become way too comfortable. She didn't want to move; didn't want the night to end. It was as if she was glued to the seat. As Vince pulled the car into the spot next to Sasha's car, they sat there for a moment in silence, simply absorbing the sexy words of the song.

Will Downing sang "I Want to Be Closer to You," and Sasha hung on every word. She wondered how he had slipped into her heart and found those very appropriate words to sing. How could he know what she was feeling at that moment?

Vince broke the silence, softly saying, "Thank you for a lovely evening."

"I had a good time," Sasha spoke. "I enjoyed dinner and the game."

"When can I see you again?"

"When would you like to?" Sasha asked. *Why don't we just sit here forever?*

"How about tomorrow?" Vince asked. "I'll make you dinner."

"Oh, I forgot…you dabble a little in the kitchen."

"Yes, I do," Vince stated proudly. "What's your favorite?"

"Surprise me," said Sasha. She was becoming accustomed to Vince's surprises and found them to be enchanting.

"You're learning to trust me," Vince said. "I'm relieved."

"Don't disappoint me." Sasha smiled. She was already falling for the handsome man she'd gotten to know only a few days before. He was quickly working his way into her heart and stealing things that had been locked away for years.

Vince grabbed her hand and slowly and gently kissed every finger. "I'll do my best not to disappoint you, Sasha Winters."

He got out of the car and moved quickly around to the passenger side to open her door. She stepped out and hit the power locks on her car. He swung her driver's door open and stood in front of it, then grabbed Sasha's waist and pulled her close. His lips gently kissed hers as he held her. She could've stayed that way forever—in Vince's strong arms. He stepped aside and allowed her to get into the car. Without another word, he shut her door and moved back toward the Corvette. Sasha pulled away, wondering why she couldn't just stay and why the night had to end so soon.

She sat with her back against the headboard. Instead of her usual sweats and T-shirt, she'd dug deep into her chest of drawers and opted for one of the sexy nighties that she rarely wore. As she sipped on a glass of Chardonnay, she went over the details of the night and relived every delightful moment. She couldn't wait to see Vince again.

Chapter 14

Scott Sanders was a gray-haired man and always well-groomed. He wore a tailored suit for every occasion. He was charming, but uncompromising in business affairs. By the time Sasha had arrived at the upscale Italian restaurant for their lunch meeting, Scott had already ordered a bottle of Chianti.

"I hope you don't mind," he said. "I ordered a celebratory bottle of wine."

"What are we celebrating?" Sasha smiled at her new client.

"Our new relationship," Scott said. "I like Louis—he's a wonderful guy—but you're so much prettier. And you come well recommended."

"Well, thank you, Mr. Sanders…"

"Call me Scott. I have a feeling we're going to become great friends." He poured her a glass of Chianti before pouring one for himself.

He held his glass in the air.

"A toast," he said.

Sasha tapped her glass against his in a toast. She didn't drink her wine, as she made it a rule not to imbibe with clients during business meetings.

"Now, if we can just get down to business." Sasha opened her iPad and pulled up her calendar. "I have us on the court's docket for the twentieth. I'd like to just go over the details of the case with you. If you can just briefly describe the events that took place concerning your terminated employee, Ralph Falkins..." She punched a few keys on her iPad.

"Ralph was one of our drug sales reps, and honestly, his work had become subpar."

"Had you spoken to him about his subpar work?"

"You have to understand the nature of our office. It's fast-paced...and competitive." Scott seemed to avoid her question.

Sasha tried a different approach. "He worked for ProTek for four years before he was terminated. He received favorable performance ratings in the past. What changed in his work performance?"

"Can I just be frank with you, Miss Winters?"

"Call me Sasha. And yes, you may be frank."

"Sasha, we have several physician partners. They recommend our products to their patients, and we compensate them extremely well for doing so. Our sales reps have to be very rigorous in their marketing techniques. Their job is to keep our numbers up—ensure that our physicians are consistently recommending our products."

"And Mr. Falkins failed to do that?"

"He had become...well...unenergetic."

"I see." Sasha punched a few more keys on her iPad,

capturing every detail. "Mr. Falkins claims that he was wrongfully terminated because he refused to engage in unscrupulous activity. Is there any truth to that claim?"

"We believe in our products, Sasha. But sometimes the process of obtaining FDA approval is cumbersome, and in some cases downright impossible. And so we have to improvise, if you know what I mean."

"Yes, I think I do know what you mean, Scott. But let me be very frank with you, as well. I am great at what I do, but I have a reputation of being an ethical attorney with high standards. If you know what I mean…" She smiled.

"Clearly," said Scott. "Do you think this guy has a chance?"

"I need everything you can dig up on his work performance. I want to know if and when he's done anything disreputable. I'd also like to review his personnel records that document any broken employment agreements."

"I'll get someone on it right away." Scott punched the keys on his smartphone as if he was giving instructions to someone.

"I'll formulate a response to his attorney." Sasha shut her iPad case and gave the menu a quick glance.

"I have to admit, before this meeting I was feeling a little nervous about your capabilities. But now I feel very safe in your hands, Sasha."

"I'm glad, Scott. You have nothing to worry about."

Sasha ordered a salad—something light. Suddenly she was cognizant of her weight and decided that she could stand to lose a few pounds. In fact, she'd wiped the dust from her treadmill just this morning and vowed to do a mile or two before bed. Her hips could stand to be toned a bit. Exercise was something that had taken a back burner in her life, but now she'd decided that it needed to be a priority.

Her lunch meeting with Scott Sanders had been successful. She was able to relieve his anxieties about the case and make the attorney transition smooth. She knew that defending ProTek wouldn't be a walk in the park, but she wasn't an ordinary attorney. She knew how to negotiate and usually was very successful in getting what she wanted—inside the courtroom and out. And this case would be no different. She'd devote all of her attention to this one.

It had been years since Sasha left work on time. She was usually the one who turned off the lights. But tonight, a very handsome man was preparing a home-cooked meal for her—something she hadn't had in a long time. She'd become too accustomed to Chinese takeout and leftovers from expensive restaurants. A home-cooked meal would be a welcome treat.

She typed Vince's address into her GPS and headed for Stone Mountain. His home was warm and inviting and filled with character—from the polished hardwood to the wooden staircase and the custom kitchen cabinets. It felt like home, unlike her place, which was cold and uninviting. She'd expected a bachelor's pad, a macho atmosphere, but what she found was anything but. His place was very manly, yet charming.

"Come in," Vince urged with a kiss to her cheek. "You look good."

"Thank you." She took a look around. Candles burned on the dining room table, and two place settings were neatly set. "Something smells really good. What's on the menu?"

"Meat loaf, mashed potatoes, corn bread…"

"Wow, you cooked all that?" she asked.

"You said you wanted a home-cooked meal. I cooked everything except for the greens."

"You got greens?"

"Yes."

"How did you manage to get greens that you didn't cook?"

"There's a little soul food place on MLK called Busy Bee Café…got the best collard greens in Atlanta. I stopped there on my way home from the office."

"I see."

"I covered all bases." Vince wrapped his arms around Sasha's waist and pulled her close. "I even took care of dessert."

"And what would that be?"

"Banana pudding for you, and a little bit of Sasha for me." He grinned and then kissed her lips.

His kiss was gentle yet passionate, and the intensity of it had her head spinning. She'd fantasized about him so many times. She kept replaying their night of passion in her head, trying to remember what it was like, but she knew that memories were nothing like the real thing.

"Let's eat before we get carried away," Vince said and then grabbed Sasha by the hand. He led her to the dining room table and pulled her chair out. "Just have a seat, madam, and I'll get you served."

Vince disappeared into the kitchen and returned with dishes filled with piping-hot food. He prepared her plate generously and then placed heaping portions onto his own plate before taking a seat across from her. They made small talk during dinner, and by the night's end, Sasha and Vince were curled up on his sofa watching a rented movie from Blockbuster. His arms were wrapped tightly around her as she leaned her head back against his chest. His chin rested atop her head. Neither of them moved a muscle long after the credits had gone up.

"I wish you'd stay the night," Vince finally said. "I would really hate to see you drive all the way across town this late."

"I didn't bring any extra clothes."

"I'll give you a shirt to sleep in," he said, "and I have a guest bedroom or you can just take my bed. I'll sleep right here."

"That's sweet, but I really have to go."

Sasha gathered herself. She could've stayed in Vince's arms all night. It felt as if she belonged there. She tried not to think about the long drive ahead of her, but she knew she had to go. It was important that she keep her feelings and hormones intact—they needed to be on the same page with her mind, and at the moment everything was out of whack.

She stood and collected her things. Vince walked her to the car, and once she was securely in she took off. At least three times before she left his subdivision she considered turning around—thought of taking that guest bedroom after all. But her good sense overruled her body and she headed home.

Chapter 15

The plan had been to meet at IHOP for a quick breakfast with the girls and then to spend the entire Saturday at the outlet mall. It had been eons since the women spent their entire Saturday together—shopping, visiting a spa or hanging out at the Cheesecake Factory for hunks of the cream cheese-flavored goodness. They'd spent many a Saturday at the bookstore, thumbing through the pages of whichever popular novel had come out that week, or placing a fillet of salmon on the barbecue grill in Sasha's backyard while sipping on mojitos. Once upon a time, Saturdays with the girls had been a standing event on Sasha's calendar. She didn't compromise when it came to that day. Whatever came up had to be rescheduled.

By the time Bridget showed up for breakfast, Sasha and their cousin Vanessa had already snagged a booth in the crowded restaurant and flipped through the menu.

Their server, Freda, had greeted them with a bright smile and her spiel regarding the specials of the day. Freda was an older woman with her hair slicked back into a ponytail. Her smock looked as if she'd been fighting in someone's kitchen, with all sorts of stains on the front of it.

"I swear you're going to be late for your own funeral," Sasha told her sister when she finally managed to drag into the restaurant.

"I'm not really feeling breakfast these days. Wish we could've just skipped it," Bridget said. She looked exhausted.

"What's going on with you, girl?" asked Vanessa. "You're not looking yourself."

"I don't feel like myself either," said Bridget. "It feels as if something, or someone, has taken over my body." Sasha hadn't shared Bridget's news with anyone. She wanted her to reveal her pregnancy to everyone in her own time.

"I'm with child." Bridget just blurted it out. It was as if she'd simply said, "I got a manicure this morning." She turned to Freda and said, "I'll have a glass of orange juice, please. And if you have some soda crackers on hand that I can nibble on, that would be great, too."

"Just regular old saltines?" Freda asked. She was a lot younger than her face revealed. She smiled innocently, but the hard lines on her face told a different story.

"Yes, just regular old saltines," Bridget mocked the woman, who had been nothing but customer friendly.

When Freda was out of earshot, Vanessa revisited Bridget's comment. "So you're preggers already? You've only been married like a millisecond!"

"Well, things happen," Bridget stated.

Vanessa's posture changed. She went into *I'm just*

an innocent bystander mode and said, "As long as you guys are both happy, then I'm happy for you."

"I'm happy," Bridget stated nonchalantly, then added, "Derrick doesn't know about it."

"What, Bridget!" Sasha exclaimed. "You still haven't told him yet?"

"I'm going to, Sasha. I just haven't had time. It's been a crazy week. I planned on doing it the day we got back from the Bahamas. Instead, he spent half the night watching Monday night football with his friends. So that didn't happen. And I've been extremely busy this week at the boutique! I'm still playing catch-up and I've been so exhausted. I've never felt fatigue like this before. I just want to sleep all the time. By the time Derrick gets in from the office at night, I'm already well spent."

"You have to make time to tell him this, Bridge. This is not something you keep from your husband!"

"I know, I know. You sound like your mother." Bridget grabbed her sister's glass of water and drank it in one gulp.

"Sure, you can have my water," Sasha said sarcastically.

Freda brought saltine crackers along with plates filled with pancakes and sausages for Sasha and Vanessa. She placed them all on the table and asked, "Is there anything else I can bring you ladies?"

"Yes," said Bridget, "can you bring me my orange juice, please? The juice that I ordered, and a glass of water? No, how about a pitcher of water?"

"Sure," Freda said, "anything else?"

"No," said Bridget.

Freda didn't seem like one to be sassed. The jailhouse tattoos on her muscular arms were a good indication of that. Sasha wanted to explain this point to Bridget, who was obviously hormonal, but it was no use.

"Thirsty, are we?" Vanessa asked after Freda disappeared.

"I feel dehydrated," Bridget said and then smiled. "So, Sasquatch. Have you told Vanessa *your* little secret?"

Sasha was puzzled. "What's my little secret?"

"Vince, of course."

"Derrick's friend?" Vanessa asked.

Before she could get it out, Bridget had already run with it. "Sasha was seen around the resort in the Bahamas with him. Somebody even said they saw you two running in the rain together. What the hell was that?"

"People should mind their own business," Sasha warned.

"Also—" Bridget took to eating Sasha's ice out of her glass "—you were seen leaving his condo at an ungodly hour of the morning."

Vanessa and Bridget stared at Sasha. They were awaiting her response to the accusations. Sasha felt embarrassed and flustered. Had someone really seen her leaving Vince's place? And if so, who?

"What is going on, Sasha Winters?" Vanessa asked.

She waited for Freda to leave from dropping off Bridget's orange juice and pitcher of water. She poured maple syrup on her pancakes while she thought of something to say. She was at a loss for words, so she went to attorney mode. "I don't know how to answer that." When in a pinch, you play crazy.

"You answer it with the truth!" Bridget said.

Sasha found herself blushing uncontrollably.

"So, you were leaving his condo at an ungodly hour," Vanessa resolved. Sasha's face was a dead giveaway.

In her best Cuban accent, Bridget imitated Desi Arnaz from the *I Love Lucy* show. "Lucy, you got some 'splaining to do."

"Start from the beginning, sister. I want every little dirty detail." Vanessa pointed her finger in Sasha's face. "I already know that Vince is Derrick's best friend... and I know that he likes to run in the rain."

"Allegedly likes to run in the rain. We can't say for certain. That's hearsay." Bridget giggled and so did Vanessa.

Sasha didn't find it humorous that someone had been spying on them. She felt a bit violated, in fact. She pointed her long finger at Bridget. "She's the one who sent him to pick me up at the airport in the first place. Why didn't she come herself or tell me to catch a taxi?"

She asked Vanessa these things as if Bridget wasn't sitting there.

"I was trying to help you out, girlfriend." Bridget was on the defensive. "I didn't want my sister trampling around aimlessly in an unknown place. I couldn't get away, and Vince offered to help."

"Okay, so he's helpful," said Vanessa as if she was keeping a checklist of Vince's attributes.

"As soon as we get in the car together, we're going at it," Sasha explained.

"Really? A lover's quarrel within the first hour of meeting," Vanessa teased. "That's not good."

"He's arrogant and cocky...yet, sweet and charismatic, all at the same time."

"So he's schizophrenic." Vanessa added that to her checklist, as well.

"And he's fine as hell," Bridget added. "But I told her from the beginning that he wasn't her type. He's not as serious about his career as you are, Sasha."

"Interpretation—he doesn't make enough money," Sasha explained. "That's Bridget's opinion of him."

"Which is why I offered to introduce you to Paul, Derrick's well-to-do friend. He comes with benefits."

"I'm not interested in Paul's benefits," Sasha said through clenched teeth.

"Okay, time-out." Vanessa formed her hands into the letter T. "Let's fast-forward. Please explain to me why you were coming out of this man's condo at an ungodly hour."

"We hit it off, okay? I like him."

"If your mother had seen you coming out of that man's room," said Bridget, "it would not have been pretty."

The three of them laughed. It was the one thing they all agreed on.

"Charlotte Winters would've had a cow," Vanessa said. "You'd be at church every Sunday for sure."

"And Wednesday night bible study too," Bridget added.

"I'm so proud of you, girl. And happy for you, Sash," said Vanessa. "You met someone nice."

"Someone who can give you some babies," Bridget added.

"And rub your feet at night." Vanessa smiled like a proud mother. "When are you bringing him to Sunday dinner?"

"I don't know. I might ask him to come for Thanksgiving."

"Oh, that would be nice, Sasha. And smart," said Bridget. "Introduce him to all of your dysfunctional relatives early. That way there's no surprises. That's what I did with Derrick."

"You're insane," Sasha told Bridget with a chuckle.

Sasha couldn't remember the last time she'd gone out for breakfast. Saturday mornings, which had been filled with hearty breakfasts and yard sales, had become a thing of the past. Sasha had become a hopeless workaholic. Over the past few years, she'd slowly worked her way into a shell—distant from everything and everyone who was healthy and right. And now, she was slowly finding her life again, and it felt good.

Chapter 16

A small space had been transformed into an office. With boxes stacked against the wall and faded wallpaper hanging on the walls, you'd swear it was nothing more than a storage room. A chair, stool and other dental equipment were the only indication that someone performed root canals and extractions in the space. Sasha wondered why Vince had chosen to operate his business in a cramped room given by a nonprofit agency—providing virtually free services to people when he could own a successful practice in the suburbs, where people would pay top dollar for his skills.

"If I don't fix the teeth of the children and elderly in our community, no one else will," Vince explained when Sasha asked.

"What about your own livelihood?"

"I make a nice living. My father left me well put. He left me a trust when he died, and I made some smart investments. The nonprofit agency pays me a small salary, but I'm not here for the money."

It was a beautiful Sunday afternoon and Vince had invited Sasha to his office to take a look around. She'd normally have gone into her own office for a few hours—prepared legal documents or returned some emails—but this Sunday had been different. He'd convinced her to meet him for brunch at one of his favorite spots, Gladys Knight and Ron Winans' Chicken and Waffles. Sasha couldn't remember the last time she'd had chicken and waffles.

She and Vince hadn't spoken in a few days. Not since he'd tried convincing her to spend the night with him.

"I won't touch you. Unless you want me to," he'd stated.

She'd wanted him to touch her all right, but she hadn't admitted it. Not to him. In her mind, she'd yearned for him. But she'd concocted the idea that before they knew each other carnally again, they needed to define their relationship. Were they just having fun or in a relationship? Were they moving toward something meaningful or merely living in the moment? These were answers that she needed from Vince, but she wasn't quite ready to ask them yet. And she wasn't quite ready to spend the night at his place.

"What you do is admirable, Vince. I'm not sure that I could do it, but it's admirable. Says a lot about your character," said Sasha.

"I think you could do it. You have a heart for people. I can just tell."

"I have a heart for people, but I'm also very high maintenance. I like my posh office and my nice salary."

"But those things aren't a necessity. Are you happy? I mean, do you really enjoy working at that law firm, or do you do it for the office and salary? Is it fulfilling? At the end of the day, are you changing lives?"

"Sure I am. I'm changing lots of lives."

"I don't mean getting people off the hook for immoral or illegal things that they've done. I mean, are you really, truly helping someone?"

Sasha pondered the question, and she couldn't truthfully answer it. She couldn't think of one single person whom she'd helped in a long time. In the beginning, when she was a law student and during her years as a junior associate, the cases were simpler and more fulfilling. Though they were cases that the firm had deemed insignificant, Sasha had been passionate about them. She even recalled a case where a woman had been discriminated against while trying to rent an apartment. She'd gone to bat for the woman and actually got her a settlement. The landlord ended up settling out of court.

Vince was right. She did have a heart for people. She was a lot like her father. Brian Winters had the warmest heart of anyone Sasha had ever known. When she was a little girl, she'd watched him take the coat off his back in the middle of winter and hand it to a homeless man in downtown Atlanta while Sasha and her sister looked on from the car. He'd arranged for her and Bridget to volunteer at food kitchens and shelters over the years— hoping to teach them a thing or two about selflessness. Toward the end of his career, he'd been accused by his firm of underbilling his attorney's fees for clients he'd grown fond of.

It was her father who had ignited the fire that she had for the law. She remembered accompanying him to the office, and she'd gone to court with him a few times. It was in those courtrooms that she'd decided to become a lawyer.

"Have a seat. Let me give you a cleaning," said Vince.

"Right now?"

"As good a time as any."

Sasha took a seat in Vince's chair, and he placed a small cape around her chest. He adjusted the seat so that it reclined and Sasha's eyes were facing the ceiling. He stood close, his cologne dancing across her nose as he caressed her face with his fingertip.

He ordered her to open her mouth. "Let me take a look-see," he said.

Opening wide and closing her eyes, Sasha hoped her teeth weren't too bad off.

"Mmm-hmm," he hummed. "I see."

"What?"

"Okay. Yes."

"Are they bad?" she asked in a panic.

"I see a cavity forming back there," he said.

"Those darn Hershey's Kisses. I can't get enough of them," she playfully admitted.

"So you have a sweet tooth for kisses, do you?"

"Yes, Hershey's Ki…"

Before she could get the last word out, Vince's lips were pressed against hers—kissing them gently. His tongue explored her mouth as she attempted to catch her breath. She closed her eyes and gently touched his face; caressed it.

"I'm sorry…didn't mean to interrupt," said a strong male voice.

Startled, Sasha sat up straight, looked toward the door and noticed a familiar face.

"Otis." Vince regained his composure and strolled toward the door and offered the man a handshake. "What are you doing here?"

"I was walking by and saw your car out front." Otis held on tightly to the hand of a young girl.

"You remember Sasha," Vince stated.

"Hard to forget such a beautiful face." Otis flashed a nice set of teeth. "Good to see you again."

"And this is Taja." Vince grinned and then reached behind the girl's ear. He pulled a quarter from somewhere and handed it to her. She seemed bored with his magic trick.

"I already know how you did that," she stated. "You pulled it from your sleeve."

"You think I just keep quarters in my sleeve?" Vince asked.

"I looked it up on the internet. I found step-by-step instructions on how the trick is performed," Taja explained.

"The internet is destroying the minds of our children, man," Vince said to Otis.

"She's too smart for her own good." Otis laughed.

"And I'm too old for that magic trick anyway. You showed me that one when I was six and a half, Dr. Sullivan. I'm eight now."

"Wow, she's eight now." He turned to Sasha as if Taja had just made a huge revelation.

"I tried getting by here on Friday," Otis explained, "but taking three buses from downtown—anyway, I didn't make it in time."

"Three buses. Why are you riding the bus? Where's your car?"

"Um…" Otis looked embarrassed. "It's been rough for me, man. Lost my car, and now we're sleeping on my buddy's couch."

"Man, I'm sorry."

"Hard to make ends meet with no income. Unemployment won't kick in for a few weeks. And even then, my former employer is fighting my unemployment."

"Is that attorney still on your case?"

"He wanted more money than I could afford to pay him. I depleted my savings when I hired him. And then he tells me that I don't have much of a case. Said he wasn't sure we could go up against a company like that. Nobody wants to go up against these big companies, man."

"Couldn't he have told you that before he took your money?"

"It was highway robbery, but what can you do? You move forward." Otis managed a smile. "Anyway, I didn't come here to bring you down. I know you don't work on Sundays, Doc, but I wanted you to know why Taja missed her cleaning. Hopefully we can reschedule."

"Now's as good a time as any," Vince said. "Sasha, do you mind letting this young lady have your seat?"

"Not at all." Sasha hopped out of the dental chair.

"Are you sure, man? We can come back another time. We don't want to intrude on your Sunday afternoon..." said Otis.

"It's fine. Besides, we wouldn't want these teeth to go another day with all that gook and grime on them. I know she's been chewing bubble gum and eating all sorts of things she shouldn't be eating," Vince teased.

Taja sat in Vince's chair. "You know I haven't been eating any candy or chewing bubble gum. You're being silly, Dr. Sullivan."

Taja's teeth were beautiful and cavity free. Vince had been her dentist since she was four years old, and he'd taught her how to care for her teeth. She'd been very methodical about the process. While most youngsters were less concerned about their teeth and more concerned about the sweet things that destroyed them, Taja took great pride in hers.

"Let me take a look," Vince said. "Open up."

Taja opened her mouth wide. "Ahhh."

"Looks good in there."

While Vince cleaned the teeth of one his favorite young patients, Sasha looked on with admiration. He was a natural with the kids, she thought. That was one of the many things that impressed her.

"So what are you going to do about your legal issues?" Vince directed his attention toward Otis again.

"I don't know, man. It's an uphill battle."

"If I might ask…what are your legal issues?" Sasha asked. "I'm an attorney. Maybe I can offer some insight."

"I'm broke." Otis smiled and held his hands in the air as if to surrender. "I can't pay for your legal advice."

Sasha smiled. "This one's on me."

"I worked for a big pharmaceutical company. Eighteen years I worked for them. One of their best salesmen. I could sell a slab of barbecue ribs to a woman wearing white gloves." Otis laughed at his own comment.

"Now, that's a good salesman." Vince laughed, too.

"They started doing unethical things. Wanted us to push drugs that hadn't been approved by the feds. When they asked me to push a particular antiseizure drug, I couldn't do it. My granddaughter here has epilepsy—since she was a toddler. How would I look pushing a drug that could potentially harm her—or other children suffering from the same disease? She's all I have. Her mother, my daughter, died while giving birth to her. My wife and I raised Taja since she was a newborn.

After my wife passed away last year, I was left to care for Taja by myself. I can't risk losing her."

"I understand," said Sasha.

"I refused to sell anything that wasn't approved by the FDA."

"Do you have anything in writing where you were asked to market the drugs?"

"Yes," Otis said. "Emails, text messages from my supervisor. I even have a doctor who is willing to testify that he was asked to push the same drug to his patients. The company offered financial rewards to him."

"And what were the actions taken against you for refusing to market the drugs."

"I was terminated."

"And what was their reason for termination?"

"They claimed that my work wasn't up to par. And that I took unauthorized time off when my granddaughter was sick."

"Did you take unauthorized time off?"

"I was told not to worry about it. Taja had an episode about two months ago. A really bad one. She was hospitalized. When I called my superior, Ron Goodman, from the hospital, he told me not to worry…said he'd take care of it. Told me to focus on making sure Taja was well, and to take as much time as I needed. Then after the fact, they used it against me."

Sasha glanced at Taja. When she first laid eyes on the girl, she appeared so healthy. She'd have never guessed that such a smart, vibrant young lady suffered from epilepsy. Her heart went out to her. But she knew she couldn't let her emotions get involved. As an attorney, she practiced the art of remaining detached. It was better that way.

"Have you had any contact with anyone at the company since you were terminated?"

"I called a million times, asking to speak with the head guy over there. I called him because I wanted some answers, but he wouldn't take my calls. He's a spineless man," Otis claimed. "That company was my life. My bread and butter for so long. I couldn't believe that I'd been let go…just like that, and without warning. I still can't believe it."

She reached into her purse and pulled out a business card. "Why don't you give me a call on Monday. I might have a colleague who can possibly take the case. She owes me a favor, so maybe I can talk her into a payment arrangement or even taking the case pro bono."

Otis reached for the card and took a long look at it before placing it into his wallet. He pulled out one of his own business cards and handed it to her.

"It's old," he explained. "Of course I don't work there anymore, but it's got my cell number on there."

Sasha read the tattered card. *Ralph Otis Falkins. Senior Sales Rep. ProTek Pharmaceuticals.* Her mind went blank for a moment. She was sure that her face had turned white when she discovered that Otis was the employee who had been terminated by her client. Was she really representing the people who had turned this man's life upside down? Was Scott Sanders responsible for Otis and his granddaughter living on the street? She felt trapped in an uncomfortable position and wished she hadn't opened this awful can of worms. Wished she could shut it.

Her mind began racing a mile a minute. How could she possibly face this man in court and stare into his eyes from across the courtroom? It would appear as if she'd just used him to gather information about his case.

And she'd be using it against him. She knew she had to end the conversation quickly.

"Call me first thing tomorrow morning," she said.

"I will, Miss Winters. Thank you." He gave her a warm, sincere smile. "You don't know how much this means to me."

"I think I do," she said.

"Well," Vince exclaimed and removed the cape from Taja's neck. "I think we're all done here, young lady."

"Yes!" Taja said and then hopped down.

"Will I see you at practice on Tuesday?"

"Of course!" she stated. "If my grandpa can get me there. We don't have a car anymore."

"Don't worry about it. I'll pick you up," said Vince.

Taja was Vince's starting guard for his coed basketball team. She was faster than most of the boys on the team and could shoot better too.

"Doc, you don't have to do that…" Otis said. "We don't want to take you out of your way."

"It's not a problem. I pick up half the team anyway. We'll just make room for one more."

"Man, I really appreciate you, Dr. Sullivan." Otis reached for Vince's hand. "And you too, Miss Winters. God bless you both."

"My pleasure," Vince said. "Any way I can help, you let me know."

Otis was near tears but quickly regained his composure. "Sasha, it was a pleasure seeing you again. And I'll be calling you on Monday."

"Good seeing you, too. And I wish you the best with your case."

"Thank you. We'll get out of your hair. Sorry to impose on your day…"

"Can we drop you somewhere?" Vince asked.

"No, no…we're going for a bite to eat when we leave here. We'll be fine."

"You sure?"

"Positive. You've done enough already." Otis grabbed Taja's hand. "Let's go, sweetheart."

"Goodbye, Dr. Sullivan." Taja grinned. "It was nice seeing you, Miss Sasha."

"Nice seeing you too, Taja. Take care of those teeth."

Taja smiled. "I will."

As the pair walked out the door, sadness overtook Sasha. She took a seat while Vince straightened his office and put equipment away. She felt defeated. In the car, she buckled her seat belt and couldn't seem to get Otis and Taja out of her mind, and the fact that she was about to help rob him of his life. The ProTek case was an important one, and she needed it. Yet, Otis's case was an important one too. His livelihood depended on the outcome.

"What you did for Otis, that was a good thing," Vince told her.

"I didn't do anything really. Just promised to get ahold of an old friend."

"It was more than he was expecting on a Sunday afternoon. It meant a lot that you even took the time to hear his plight."

"It was nothing."

"You listened to his legal troubles and offered to help him go after the scumbag that fired him," Vince said, and added, "See, you do have a heart."

"I know I have a heart." Sasha smiled too.

"It would be a wonderful thing if your friend can take the case," said Vince. "If she can't, couldn't you represent Otis?"

"It's not that simple," she said.

"Oh, right. I almost forgot...you work for that big glitzy law firm downtown where they bill you for every little thing. He can't afford you," Vince mused. "How much would something like that cost, anyway?"

"You mean his legal fees?"

"Yes. Say he had a friend who wanted to help out with the costs?"

"Even if he could afford me, I can't take on any new cases right now."

She couldn't bring herself to tell Vince the truth—that she wasn't able to take Otis's case because she was already representing the scumbag who fired him.

"Okay, I understand. At least I tried, right?" Vince said.

"Yes." Sasha felt as if she'd betrayed a friend.

When she and Vince turned the corner on Decatur Street, they passed the huge Catholic church that stood strong and tall with its tan-colored brick and beautiful architecture. She watched as Otis and Taja stood in the long line at the food kitchen. Her heart sank.

Chapter 17

Sasha flipped open a law book and traced her index finger along the page until she found the exact reference that she needed for her case. She took a sip of her latte and leaned back into her chair. Thoughts of Vince filled her head. She seemed to think of him more often than not, and she wondered if he thought of her just as much. She suddenly had a visual of his beautiful chocolate-colored chest—the curve of his muscles like chocolate mountains. She smiled at the thought.

When Keira buzzed her, she was instantly thrown back into reality.

"Robin Hayes is on line one."

"Thanks," said Sasha and then picked up the call. "It's Sasha Winters."

"Sasha! It's been too long, girl."

"Robin, hey!"

"I got your message about that case with the guy

who was wrongfully terminated from that pharmaceutical company."

"Can you take it?"

"No can do, honey. I'm out of the country. Taking a much-needed sabbatical. I'll be in Africa for another month or so."

"It must be nice being you. You lead such a fabulous life!" Sasha said.

"You could too, girl, if you'd just let yourself go once in a while." Robin laughed. "Kyle Johnson has this awful hold on you. You'd think the two of you were married or something."

Sasha was quiet—she knew that Robin's words were true. Although she'd been afraid to admit it, Kyle and the firm did have a hold on her. Robin was never one to bite her tongue; she always said exactly what she believed was the truth—and said it in a very no-nonsense manner.

"You're smart enough to have your own practice," Robin continued. "Hell, the two of us could go into business together and smash our adversaries. Picture it—two beautiful, brilliant attorneys who love the law. Nothing could stop us, except for our own inhibitions. And you know I don't have any of those. You should think about it."

Robin, who had been Sasha's classmate in college and in law school, had always been someone she had great respect for. She was a beautiful dark woman with a thick mountain of natural hair. She was a brilliant lawyer. Robin had worked as an intern for a law firm for a short time after college but soon had started her own practice. She was too proud and strong-willed to work for anyone else. Robin was a free spirit, and over the years, Sasha had secretly wished she could be more like her.

"I want to hear all about Africa when you get back." Sasha completely disregarded Robin's comments about going into private practice. Something like that required her to let go of her safety net—something she wasn't quite willing to do yet.

"Sorry I couldn't help with your friend. I think he has a good case, and should pursue the scumbags that fired him with full force! Why don't you take the case yourself?"

"Conflict of interest," Sasha said hesitantly. "I'm actually representing the scumbags that fired him."

"Wow, Sasha! You've gotten yourself into a mess," said Robin. "But you're smart and you have a good heart. You'll figure it out. In the meantime, I want to know what's going on with you socially, but these international fees are killing me. So email me!"

"I will, Robin," said Sasha. "Enjoy Africa! And I'll be in touch."

"Good! We're doing lunch the minute I'm back in Atlanta. I haven't had sushi in so long, I'm having withdrawals!"

"We'll have sushi when you return. At the Atlanta Fish Market."

The Atlanta Fish Market had been their favorite place to splurge during college. Housed in a brick building inspired by a 1920s Savannah train station, the restaurant boasted some of the freshest seafood in the city. Although their prices weren't designed for broke law students on a budget, the pair had hopelessly developed an undying taste for sushi there. It was a place they'd visited so often, the servers knew them by name. A place where their friendship had blossomed into more of a sisterhood than she shared with her own sister. It was where she first met Kevin, an architecture student at Morehouse College, who bused tables there at night.

"You're on, girlfriend!" Robin exclaimed. "Let me know how your case turns out."

"I will."

"And seriously consider joining me in private practice. Tell Kyle you're not interested in being his love slave anymore."

"You are too much!" Sasha said.

"You know he's got the hots for you, right? That's why he keeps you on your toes."

"No, actually he's got the hots for Kirby, the wet-behind-the-ears attorney I trained," Sasha told her friend.

"You're sadly mistaken, honey. Kirby's just someone he has hot, lustful sex with, and he repays her for it by moving her up the ladder. But you...he's got the hots for you. But because you won't give him the time of day, he does everything humanly possible to make your life a living hell." Robin threw out her insight upon Sasha, even though it was not asked for. "He has no intentions of allowing that little girl to become partner of that firm. Are you kidding me? You have more knowledge in your baby finger than she has in her head. And he knows it."

"Where do you get this stuff from?"

"Tell that little twit that you've got a better offer, and watch how he reacts," said Robin. "Your parents doing their usual Thanksgiving celebration?"

"Yes," Sasha said. "You're coming, aren't you?"

"I should be back in the country by Thanksgiving," Robin stated. "I'll tentatively plan on being there."

"Good! Everyone will be glad to see you."

"I'll talk to you when I return, Sasha. Take care, and think about what I said."

"I will."

"Okay, sweetheart, I've gotta go. I'll see you in a bit."

"Goodbye," Sasha mumbled.

Robin was good about starting a fire and then rushing from the scene as things burned. She was frightfully intuitive, which is the characteristic that made her such a great lawyer. When Sasha first started dating Kevin, Robin had predicted that the relationship would end—and how.

"He's not it, girl. Just have a little fun, but don't get all wrapped up in him," Robin had warned about Kevin early on. "He's going nowhere fast and intends to take you with him. I don't want to see you get hurt."

Hurt is exactly where Kevin had left her.

An influenza epidemic had swept across their campus. Everyone was sick. And when Kevin suddenly canceled their date one night claiming that the flu had overtaken him, Sasha hadn't given it a second thought. The comedy club could wait, even though she'd spent over one hundred dollars on the tickets for his birthday. His health had been more important.

"Take Robin," he'd stated. "The two of you should go and have fun."

"But it's your birthday," she'd told him. "I want to spend it with you."

"I don't want you sick, babe. You've got too much going on. If we're both sick, we're no good for each other. I'll be fine in a few days. You and Robin go to the show and have a good time. I'm going to get some much-needed rest."

It sounded like a reasonable thing to do, although it didn't seem fair that he spend his birthday alone. She needed to see him—at least to drop off his gift—an Atlanta Falcons jersey that she'd picked up at the mall a few weeks before. Maybe she'd even take him a bowl of soup. It was the least she could do before heading to the show with Robin.

She made her way to the third floor of his apartment building and approached his door. A red scarf hung from the doorknob. The red scarf was a symbol used by Kevin and his roommate as an indication that one of them had a female guest in the apartment and shouldn't be disturbed. When one of them saw the red scarf, the other knew that he should go find something to do for a while and come back later.

Sasha contemplated whether or not she should knock. If Kevin's roommate, Avery, was entertaining a girl, she certainly didn't want to interrupt. She tapped lightly on the door. But no one answered. She was just about to walk away when Avery popped up out of nowhere.

"Hey, Sasha," he said. "I swear I'll be out of your hair in a minute. I just forgot to grab my laptop. Try to go easy on the birthday boy. He's got a big game tomorrow."

She didn't mention the scarf and the fact that she thought Avery was entertaining a guest in the apartment. She simply played along. "I don't know how much fun he'll be tonight or if he'll even be able to play in tomorrow's game. He's got the flu."

"Really?" Avery looked confused as he stuck his key into the lock and stepped inside the apartment. "I didn't know he was sick. Could've fooled me. He looked just fine when I saw him earlier."

Sasha followed Avery into the apartment. He quickly disappeared into his bedroom and grabbed his laptop. In a flash he was back out the door.

Sasha had a horrible feeling in her gut as she stood in their living room. A bottle of wine and two used glasses rested on the coffee table, and a pair of women's high-heeled shoes sat on the floor. She heard light moans as she slowly approached Kevin's bedroom. She already knew what to expect but slowly turned the handle anyway. Standing there, she watched in silence as the young woman's naked body mounted her man, moving up and down to the rhythm of a Luther Vandross tune. With closed eyes, Kevin kissed her mouth hungrily—he didn't notice Sasha standing there. Not at first. By the time their eyes met, her world had already fallen apart. And her face was completely drenched with tears.

He never even ran after her.

Robin had been right about Kevin. However, she'd never boasted about it but simply consoled Sasha after the first of many breakups and helped her through the pain. She'd been a true friend.

Because Robin was so outspoken, Sasha was hesitant about mentioning anything about Vince to her. Although she wanted to keep him safe from the wrath of her friend, part of her wanted to know the truth about him. She wanted to know if he really was too good to be true or if he was hiding something. The revelation would definitely save her an abundance of heartache. On the other hand, she was having such a great time with him, she couldn't think of troubling the waters.

Sasha hung up the phone and stared out the window at the building across the street. She longed for a better view but wondered if she'd ever get one. The sky was dark and the rain had already started to fall over downtown. She found herself wondering if Otis and Taja were somewhere safe from the rain. She wondered if they'd had breakfast this morning or if they'd stood in line at the food kitchen again.

She wondered how she would break the news to Otis that her friend wasn't able to take his case. She looked through her Rolodex and found the phone number for Legal Aid. Perhaps they could offer assistance. Maybe she had colleagues who could offer him a job. If Sasha put her mind to it, she knew she could possibly help Otis to get on his feet again.

Keira buzzed her again.

"Sasha, your sister's on line two."

"Thanks, Keira." Sasha picked up her phone. "What's up, Bridge?"

She heard a light whimpering on the phone.

"Bridget?" Sasha called.

"He left me, Sasha," said Bridget in between tears.

"Who left you?"

"Derrick went to stay with Vince after I told him about the baby. He said he needed some space to think," Bridget said between sobs. "I don't know what to do, Sasha."

"Where are you?"

"I'm at home." Her sister sounded as if she was falling apart. "Can you come over? I just need someone to talk to."

"I'll be right over."

"Thanks, Sasha," she said softly, and then hung up.

Sasha had never heard her sister sound like that before. Bridget was always so strong and self-assured, except when the tears were convenient. And Sasha suspected that these were real tears as she rushed down the interstate toward Bridget and Derrick's newly built home in the Cascade area. She reflected on the news that Bridget had shared with her in the Bahamas. She had secretly gotten pregnant when her husband had specifically asked her not to. Sasha knew that nothing good would come from Bridget's secret. She suddenly felt guilty for not protecting her little sister better. Had she not been so consumed with her own life and career, she could've been a better mentor for Bridget.

When Sasha first met Derrick, she knew he'd have his hands full with Bridget. It was no secret that her sister was self-absorbed and selfish and paid too much attention to the wrong things. Since that time, Derrick had endured more than his share of Bridget's antics but stuck around, and he still had asked for her hand in marriage despite everything. He was a good man, but Bridget had taken him for granted. Even as Sasha rushed to her sister's aid, she knew that Bridget had brought this upon herself.

Sasha knocked twice and then rang the bell. Bridget swung the door open. Her eyes were puffy and bright red.

"Don't judge," Bridget said.

"I'm not here to judge you." Sasha stepped into the foyer.

The home was grand, with mahogany hardwood throughout. Everything was custom; Bridget had insisted on it.

"And don't say I told you so," said Bridget.

Sasha followed Bridget into the kitchen with its huge stainless steel appliances and granite counters. She took a seat at the island and picked up a few grapes from the fruit basket on the counter.

"It's lunchtime and I'm starving," she explained.

"I'll make you a sandwich." Bridget walked over to the refrigerator and pulled out cold cuts, lettuce, tomatoes and mayonnaise. She washed her hands and opened a loaf of wheat bread.

"You're going to make me a sandwich?" Sasha asked skeptically.

She was surprised. Bridget had never made Sasha a sandwich. It was always the other way around. When they were younger, Sasha had made her sister plenty of sandwiches—peanut butter and jelly was her favorite. Bridget had never been domestic. She was great at figuring out how to get things without putting in the work.

"Of course I'm going to make you a sandwich." She sounded nasally from crying. "You want ham or pastrami?"

"Ham."

Sasha watched with amazement as her sister put together a delicious sandwich.

"I know you had to leave work, Sasha. Thank you for that. But I just really needed someone to talk to." She placed the sandwich on a small plate and slid it in front of Sasha. "As soon as I told him about the baby, he got so angry. I've never seen Derrick like that."

Sasha ate in silence. She didn't know what to say.

"He asked how far along I was and offered to pay for an abortion. Can you believe that? How could he be so cold?" She started crying again.

Sasha stood, walked around to the other side of the island and grabbed her sister. "It'll be okay, Bridge. He just needs some time to figure things out. He'll come around."

"I don't know, Sasha. He was really mad this time. He packed a lot of his things, and he didn't even say goodbye. He just walked out and slammed the door."

"Bridget, I know you don't want to hear this right now, but you have to start considering your husband's feelings. You pressured him into setting a date for the wedding, and then you moved that date up three times. He tells you he wants to buy a little loft near downtown so that he could be closer to work, but you insist on this big house with custom everything. He tells you he wants to wait two years before having children, and you completely disregard his wishes."

Bridget looked at her sister with puppy dog eyes. "He doesn't fight me on things. He lets me have my way."

"Because he loves you, silly. He's bending every single time, and you're not reciprocating. And finally he's fed up."

"You think he'll come back?"

"I don't know, Bridget. You've been married like two weeks, and you've already pushed him over the edge."

Bridget cried harder.

"I think if you really put your mind to it, you can make him come back."

"I can't go through nine months of pregnancy by myself, Sasha."

"You won't have to. I'll be right here by your side, sweetie."

"You promise?" she asked.

"I promise. I'll go to the Lamaze classes and everything."

"Seriously? You hate that kind of stuff."

"I'll go!" Sasha insisted. "Now, can I please have something to drink?"

"Of course." Bridget walked over to the refrigerator and grabbed Sasha a bottle of sweet tea.

"I love you, Sasha. I know I don't say it that often. And even though I'm always giving you a hard time, I really look up to you. You really have it together, and I wish I could be more like you."

Sasha was overcome with emotion. Her sister had never opened her heart that way. For as long as she could remember, Bridget resented her success. She resented that their father favored Sasha more. She dealt with it by magnifying Sasha's flaws and belittling her choices in life. Sasha had even suspected that Bridget wanted her to meet Paul because she knew that Vince was a better choice.

"I love you too, Bridge." Sasha gave her sister a tight squeeze. "Derrick will be back soon. This is his home, and he loves you."

"I hope you're right, Sasha."

Sasha hoped so too.

Chapter 18

After a week, Vince was up to his ears in conversations about Bridget. He'd hoped to dismiss Derrick's claims that she'd gotten pregnant on purpose and that he was never going back home, but it was no use. Derrick was convinced of it, and as a result, he was never returning. He'd start a new life; find a loft overlooking downtown. She could have that big, overpriced house in Cascade. He never wanted to buy it in the first place— it had been Bridget's dream house, not his.

Vince's house hadn't been the same since Derrick moved in. The guest bathroom was a mess, the family room was a mess, and the kitchen was worse than any other room in the house. Derrick had taken a leave of absence from his job, which left him depressed and with nothing to do all day but wallow in his grief.

Thus, leaving Vince's house in disarray.

He missed Sasha like crazy; hadn't seen her since

Derrick moved in. Wanting to be there for his friend, he'd asked her to give him some time while he helped his best friend deal with his pain. She understood and in fact was spending just as much time with her sister, consoling her. They were both busy, their lives being consumed by other people's worries. Too busy to even realize that they were slowly being absorbed into Derrick and Bridget's drama.

Well, today it would end! He'd have to put his foot down. He needed to see Sasha something terrible, and he was about to make it happen. He dialed her number and she picked up on the first ring.

"Hey, stranger." Her voice sounded like music in his ears.

"Hey, yourself. I've missed you so much. What are the chances I can see you soon?"

"I say the chances are pretty good. What did you have in mind?"

"A nice meal…a bottle of wine…a few candles…some jazz. I know a nice spot in Midtown."

"Sounds wonderful. I'm stuck in traffic, but I'm on my way home. I just need to change into something nice."

"I'll pick you up at eight."

"I'll be ready," Sasha said.

"I can't wait to see you."

"Same here."

When Vince stepped into his house, a foul odor hit his nose right away. He followed it into the kitchen, where he found dishes stacked in the sink and a two-liter bottle of soda left opened on the counter. He searched for Derrick and found him stretched out on the sofa in the family room. A pillow from the guest bedroom was beneath his head, and he was yelling obscenities at the television while watching *Judge Judy*.

"Hey, bro, what's that smell?" Vince asked him.

Derrick raised his head from the pillow just long enough to look at Vince. "Oh, I burned some popcorn."

"The kitchen is a mess. Did you happen to notice?"

"Yeah, I planned on cleaning it up after *Judge Judy* went off."

"Bro, you've got to get it together." Vince sat on the edge of the chair across from Derrick and looked him square in the eye. He was no good at beating around the bush. He was up front with him. "Man, my house is a hot mess. I don't live like this. And you…bro, you stink. I don't know when you last showered, but you really have this stench about you. And when was the last time you shaved? You're starting to look like a caveman."

Derrick sat straight up. "You want me to leave?"

"I want you to shower, bro. Run some hot water and fall underneath it. You're welcome to stay here as long as you need to. My door is always open. You know that. But you've got to stop wallowing in your self-pity. You have a woman who loves you at home. Sure, she made a mistake…"

"Not a mistake." Derrick held his finger in the air to interrupt. "Bridget knew exactly what she was doing."

"Okay, fine. Maybe she did, maybe she didn't. I don't know, but the reality is you have a kid growing inside of her now. The question is, what are you going to do about it? I've known you since the ninth grade, and you've never been the type of guy to ignore your responsibilities. You know as well as I do that you can't run from your problems, man, you have to face them."

Derrick dropped his face into his hands. "You're right, Vince. I do have to face them."

"Can't run forever. And you definitely can't live with me forever. Not like this. Man, you are fun-ky!"

"We lived together in college."

"That was different. We were both slobs back then."

Both men laughed this time. Derrick knew that Vince was telling the truth. But he'd shut down because he hadn't wanted to hear it.

"Now—" Vince stood "—I have a date with a beautiful woman tonight..."

"Sasha," Derrick said.

"Yes, Sasha."

"You like her, huh?"

"I like her a lot. I think I might even be in love with her, but that's between you and me. Can't tell a woman things like that too soon."

"I feel you."

"But in due time, I'll let her know that I think she's the one."

"I'm happy for you, bro. Sasha's got style. She's one of the good ones."

"Yes, she is. And so is Bridget. They're from the same genes, the same roots." Vince had given Derrick something to think about. "Now, if you'll excuse me, I'm going upstairs to get changed. I'm going out for a night on the town. Not sure how long I'll be gone, but when I get back I don't expect my house to look like the Tasmanian devil's been through here."

"I got you, man."

"I hope you do."

Vince danced up the stairs to his bedroom. He hit the power button on his stereo, and Frankie Beverly's voice floated through the house. He hit the shower and then quickly dressed in a pair of jeans, a tangerine colored button down shirt and tan blazer. He slipped a pair of brown loafers on his feet and splashed cologne on his neck.

Sasha had a modest home in East Marietta that overlooked the Chattahoochee River. It fit her. It looked as if a workaholic lived there, though, with plants that hadn't been watered and rooms that looked as if they'd never been used except for special occasions. Her home was neat but somewhat frigid. She, however, looked ravishing in her sexy, green dress. Her bare shoulders and lean legs had him aroused without notice. He greeted her with a strong hug and searched for her lips. Once found, he kissed them with intensity. He missed her; wanted her.

"We'd better go before I change my mind." He laughed. "Any longer and we won't be going anywhere with you looking like that."

She quickly slipped her feet into a pair of heels and grabbed a jacket. Vince made certain her front door was locked before escorting her to the car. He opened her door, and she slipped into the passenger seat of his sports car. Before long, they were breezing down the highway.

When they stepped into the elegant jazz spot, the hostess led them to the table that Vince had reserved. He ordered Sasha a glass of the house wine and a Black Russian for himself.

"Maybe I wanted a Black Russian," she teased, "or a dirty one."

"Would you like a Dirty Black Russian?" he asked.

"Yes, I would," she said.

"Excuse me, sweetheart," Vince called to the sexy

waitress. "Can you bring the lady a Dirty Black Russian instead of the wine?"

"Yes, I can." She gave Vince a flirtatious smile before sashaying away.

"Now…you remember what happened the last time you tried to drink with me, right?"

"Yes, you took advantage of me." Sasha grinned and Vince's hormones went into overdrive when he thought of the Bahamas. And when she smiled, it was as if he had never seen her smile before.

"You can't hold your liquor, so I'm giving you a limit," Vince told her.

"You can't give me a limit!" Sasha disagreed.

"Two." He laughed. "And that's it for you."

As the live band played a familiar melody, Vince took in the beauty of his date. He'd been a jazz buff for some time and knew many artists and arrangements that the average listener wouldn't recognize. When the band did a rendition of an old Michael Franks tune, "When She Is Mine," Vince sang along. The ballad's lyrics reminded him of Sasha.

He suddenly grabbed Sasha's hand and whisked her onto the dance floor. He held her close as they moved slowly to the music. She was everything he'd ever wanted. When he thought of the perfect woman, it was her face that appeared in his mind.

They spent the evening catching up on what had taken place during the week and comparing notes on Derrick and Bridget's relationship. They danced a few more times and had a few more drinks before leaving.

Back at Sasha's home, Vince grabbed the keys from her hand and unlocked the door. He stepped inside, and she followed.

"You want coffee?" she asked.

"Love some," he said and followed her into the kitchen.

He looked around. The kitchen was the most lived-in room in the house. While she brewed coffee, he moved through the house and into the formal living room, where he found a bookshelf. He browsed through her books, which were mostly law related. There were a few novels sprinkled about—works such as Zora Neale Hurston's *Their Eyes Were Watching God* and Toni Morrison's *Sula.* It was obvious she was a fan of the Harlem Renaissance poets—she had books by just about every one of them, from Langston Hughes to Marcus Garvey.

The living room had been used quite often also, he thought, but mostly for work. She rarely gave any attention to her works of fiction, if any. They'd successfully begun to collect dust.

When he heard Nina Simone's strong voice ring through the speakers, Vince knew he'd found his soul mate.

"What do you know about that music, woman?" he asked.

"I know a little something," she said and handed him a cup of coffee. "My grandfather introduced me to all of this. Duke Ellington, John Coltrane, Miles Davis, Etta James. I spent a lot of time with my grandfather. I have all of his old music."

"You're a woman after my own heart." He took a sip of java. It was perfectly sweetened.

"I'm going to change into something a little comfy," Sasha said and then disappeared.

Vince found her music collection and flipped through the tattered album covers. Sasha definitely had an old soul, and he loved it. It seemed that they had so much in common, it was scary.

"You should have these albums transferred to digital," he yelled to her from the living room.

"What?" she yelled back. "I can't hear you!"

"I said, you should have these albums…" Midway through his sentence he turned and looked at her. She wore a sexy, silk white nightie. It was knee-length and sheer. Her breasts were round and supple beneath the material. He softly finished his sentence. "You should have them transferred to digital."

She moved closer to him and placed her hands on his chest. He gently squeezed her soft breasts and kissed her lips. His hands moved to the round of her butt and caressed it softly. He slipped his shoes from his feet and Sasha helped him to remove his blazer. She carefully unbuttoned his shirt and removed it. Their lips remained together as they both fumbled with his belt buckle. He removed his jeans and his T-shirt until he was standing there in his briefs.

He was surprised when he felt Sasha's hand creep toward his inner thigh and massage him there. A burst of sensation rushed through him. He wanted her more at that moment than he remembered wanting anyone. Just as he was about to remove the sexy, flimsy material that Sasha wore, he thought he heard the doorbell ring.

"Are you expecting someone?" he whispered.

"No," she whispered back.

Vince slipped his jeans back on and pulled the T-shirt over his head. He moved toward the door. Looked through the peephole. Couldn't really see who it was, so he tried to flip on the porch light. No luck.

"It needs a bulb," Sasha explained.

"We're fixing that tomorrow," Vince ordered. In a strong, deep voice, he yelled toward the door, "Who is it?"

A soft, sweet voice said, "Sasha, it's me, Bridget."

Vince exhaled. Sasha rushed into her bedroom, grabbed a robe and wrapped it around her body. Vince stepped aside and allowed her to open the door.

"What are you doing here?" Sasha asked.

"I couldn't stay in that house one more night by myself," Bridget said as she stepped inside. "I started hearing things, and oh—" She noticed Vince standing there barely dressed. "Am I interrupting something?"

Vince gave Bridget a slight wave.

"I'm sorry, Sash. I didn't know you had company. I tried calling, but you didn't pick up."

"My phone was in my purse. Vince and I went out tonight, so I stuck it in there and forgot all about it."

"Um…where did y'all go?"

"Just a little jazz spot in Midtown."

"Was it Sambuca?" she asked and then answered her own question, "No, I think they've closed down. I'm trying to remember a jazz spot in Midtown…"

"It's a private spot," Vince explained.

"Oh."

"Sasha, I'm gonna leave," Vince said after buttoning his shirt and slipping into his blazer.

"I'm sorry, guys. I didn't mean to interrupt your evening," Bridget said. "Don't leave, Vince. Stay and finish…whatever it is you were doing. I'll be as quiet as a church mouse. You guys won't even know I'm here."

"It's late and I should be going anyway," Vince said and then walked toward the front door.

"Is Derrick okay?" Bridget asked Vince.

"He's doing just fine."

"Can you ask him to call me?"

"Sure, I'll tell him," Vince said.

"Thanks," said Bridget and then made her way toward the kitchen.

Sasha walked Vince to the door. "I'm sorry. I didn't know she was coming."

"It's okay. I had a great time tonight. Thank you for a wonderful evening."

"Thank you."

He kissed her cheek. "I'll call you tomorrow."

"Call me tonight before you go to sleep."

He dipped out the door without another word.

When Vince stepped into his house and tossed his keys on the table, the smell of Lysol and other cleaning products hit his nose immediately. He went into the kitchen to grab a glass of water before turning in for the night. The dishes had been cleaned and put away and the granite counters were sparkling. Vince removed his blazer and his shirt as he walked upstairs. Outside the guest bedroom door stood two large suitcases and a smaller bag; Derrick's luggage had been packed. He was leaving, and Vince was happy about that. The door was ajar, so Vince peeked inside. Derrick lay peacefully across the bed, sound asleep. Loud snores echoed through the house—those same snores that had caused Vince a week's worth of sleepless nights.

He made his way down the hall and into his own bedroom, sat on the edge of the bed and removed his watch and jewelry. He reminisced about Sasha wearing that sexy nightgown. She'd displayed the audacity that he knew she had within her. She'd looked so sexy in the flimsy material. A bolt of lightning had rushed through him when he'd set eyes on her, and when she'd touched him he'd lost all sense of time.

He definitely loved her. No ifs, ands or buts about it. And the first chance he got, he was going to let her know.

Chapter 19

At dawn, Sasha stepped outside with her robe pulled tight. She grabbed her morning paper and then rushed back into the house. The chill made her shiver. The leaves on the trees had already transformed into bright shades of red, yellow and orange. She loved autumn in Atlanta. It was her favorite time, with its cool mornings and mild afternoons. When she and Bridget were younger, their family spent long weekends in the north Georgia mountains—camping, hiking and fishing with their father. It was those times in her life that she remembered and enjoyed most—sipping hot chocolate in front of a warm fire. Those times were simpler.

She thought of Taja, a little girl being raised by her grandfather. Grandfathers weren't particularly equipped to raise young girls. Girls needed a woman's hand to guide them. They needed the gentleness and the wisdom that came along with it. She'd have questions soon that her grandfather wouldn't have the answers to. Her body would change, and she'd enter puberty way sooner than anyone could prepare her for. It was true Otis didn't have all the tools Taja needed, but Sasha loved his commitment to her. She could clearly see that he loved his granddaughter. And sometimes, that was enough.

It was the same type of love her father had for her— the kind that moved mountains. He'd make a way when there was no path in sight. He would provide a warm place to sleep and a sufficient meal, and all the things a man needed to care for his child. For Otis, ProTek had taken so much from him; left him helpless. It had taken away his power to move mountains for his granddaughter. Sasha had the power to change things for them.

She spread her newspaper out on the table. When she had time to read the *Atlanta Journal Constitution,* she did so from front to back. She usually perused it during her short lunch break while sitting at her desk. But this morning she took her time. She rarely delayed getting into the office; she was always punctual. There was usually some fire that awaited her every morning, and she rushed into the office just to put it out. But this morning was different. She enjoyed those precious early morning hours.

Her Keurig coffeemaker hadn't been used in months, but she'd managed to dust it off and brew two perfect cups of decaf when she'd entertained Vince. She remembered how handsome he looked in orange. It was definitely his color, she thought as her mind drifted to the night's events. She'd enjoyed the jazz club immensely and had heard music that she'd never thought she would like. The two of them had danced the night away and simply enjoyed each other's company. They were as different as night and day, yet had so much in common. She'd learned so much from him in a very short time. She'd learned that life is worthless unless you follow your heart. Which is what she'd planned on doing first thing this morning.

She would remove herself from the ProTek case. A conflict of interest now existed between her and the parties in the case, and it would be unethical for her to continue to represent ProTek against Otis. There was no way she could stand in that courtroom, look into Otis's eyes and claim that he had been justly terminated by a company that didn't know the meaning of the word.

She knew that the case would undoubtedly be reassigned to Kirby, giving her rival just enough ammunition to win the battle. But it couldn't be helped. It was the right thing to do.

The next thing Sasha heard was someone moving in the hallway.

"You're up bright and early," said Bridget, wiping sleep from her eyes.

"I'm up early every morning." Sasha moved the newspaper over to pave some space at the table for Bridget to join her.

After pouring a glass of orange juice, Bridget took the seat across from Sasha at the kitchen table. "You and Vince are getting pretty cozy, huh? It looked like y'all were about to do the nasty when I showed up last night. He was breathing all hard, and you…with your little sexy nightie on underneath that robe."

"Bridget, please."

"*Bridget, please.* Is that all you have to say, girl?" She took a long drink of juice. "You know you are feeling that man. Just let go, Sasha. Let yourself be free. Take your attorney hat off and put your freak hat on!" Bridget giggled at her own comment.

"I had my freak hat on last night and then you showed up at the door." Sasha laughed.

"I knew it!" Bridget exclaimed. "I knew y'all were doing something freaky up in here."

They both laughed.

"I'm happy for you, sis. Vince is a good man and I think he makes you very happy. He tends to bring out the best in you. You're different these days. And it's a good thing."

"What's up with you today? You going to the boutique?" Sasha asked.

"Not today. Derrick's coming home," she said. "He's ready to talk."

"Really?" Sasha grabbed her sister's hand and gave it a squeeze. "That's good, Bridge. You happy about it?"

"Ecstatic!" She closed her eyes and lifted her head upward. "I've missed him so much. And I heard you the other day…about considering his feelings and stuff. I've been a horrible woman to him. I don't know how he's put up with me for so long."

"My sentiments exactly," Sasha mused.

"Anyway," Bridget said, ignoring the comment, "I'm ready to do this the right way."

"I'm happy for you, love. Go get your man!"

Before leaving the kitchen, Bridget hugged her sister's neck.

Sasha decided to take her time getting into the office. She made herself another cup of coffee and sat at her kitchen table, looking out the kitchen window and enjoying the view. The trees in her backyard displayed a kaleidoscope of autumn colors. While she was fighting tooth and nail for an office with a view, she realized that the perfect view was right here in her backyard.

Sasha had asked Keira to schedule a meeting with Kyle, and to have the ProTek file available for her. When she walked in, Keira handed her the file and her usual Frappuccino.

"Thanks for the Frap, but you don't have to get me Starbucks anymore," Sasha told her. "I'm going to have coffee at home from now on."

"Really? Good for you, Sasha Winters," Keira said. "The little short man is waiting for you."

Sasha stepped into Kyle's office. He was leaned back in his chair with his feet atop his desk. He was speaking with someone on the phone, but motioned for Sasha to take a seat. She sat with her legs crossed and waited for him to complete his phone call.

Once he was done, he looked at his watch. "You just getting here?"

"Yes."

"You're usually here earlier." He looked confused. "So what's up? You have questions about ProTek?"

"I have to remove myself from the case. There's a conflict of interest with me and one of the litigants."

"How so?"

"I know the plaintiff, and I feel that my relationship with him might conflict with the best interests of the firm's representation of ProTek. I don't feel that I can be objective in this case."

"I see. So you think that the case should be reassigned to another attorney?"

"I believe that would be best."

"You don't know what you want, do you, Sasha? One minute you're begging me for this case, the next minute you're crying about a conflict of interest. Sometimes in this field we call law, we have to do things that are a bit unethical."

Sasha stood. "No, we don't. I'm an ethical attorney, and I won't do anything that makes me uncomfortable. Now, if you'll excuse me, I have tons of work to do."

Sasha sashayed out of his office. She shut the door behind her. She felt good. Empowered.

Chapter 20

Vince paced the floor at the gym—back and forth. He was nervous. His youth basketball team was down by two points with just minutes left on the clock. He needed someone who could score, and he knew exactly who that was. Taja was his best scorer, but after the third quarter, she'd been out of breath and he wanted her to rest.

"Put me back in, Coach," she begged.

He looked over at her but continued to pace the floor, his arms folded across his chest with his finger beneath his chin.

He glanced into the stands and searched for Sasha's pretty face. She'd promised to drop by after work to check out his team. He managed to find her in the midst of the crowd. When their eyes met, she blew him a kiss and he smiled. He moved closer to the kids on the bench. Taja grabbed his hand.

"Coach," she whined, "put me in! We're down by two points. I can hit them and get fouled. They'll send me to the free throw line, and you know the rest."

She had it all worked out in her little mind. It was the same play that he'd concocted in his own thoughts just a few minutes earlier. It was as if the child had been here before.

"We can't afford to lose this game." She gave him a look with those beautiful eyes.

He glanced over at her grandfather, who was seated just behind the bench. Otis gave him a nod that said it was okay to put her in. He knew how persistent and persuasive his granddaughter could be. She was a professional negotiator, and an even better ballplayer.

Vince told her to go check in at the scorer's table. Her replacement, Josh, looked disheartened as he took his place on the bench, folding his arms across his chest in a huff.

Taja's ponytails bounced up and down as she rushed down court with the ball. When she went up for a layup, she was fouled by a boy from the other team just before the ball swished into the basket. Vince gave Otis a huge grin.

Taja stood at the free throw line and positioned herself just as Vince had taught her in practice. With a square stance and her feet shoulder-length apart, she dribbled the ball. With a quick toss, the ball went into the basket. The crowd went crazy. Vince glanced into the stands again and looked at Sasha. She was standing now and cheering. She gave him a thumbs-up, and his heart soared. He was so happy that she was there supporting something that he loved so much.

Everything had fallen right into place and Vince's team was up by one point. His players rushed down

court as the opposing team tried to make a basket before the buzzer sounded. But it was too late. The game
was over, and his team had prevailed.

Taja rushed toward her grandfather, who was standing on the sidelines waiting with open arms to give her
a celebratory hug. She stopped just two feet short and
fell to the floor with a loud thump. With her eyes roll-
ing into the back of her head, she began jerking. Vince
and Otis rushed to her side, and people began to gather
around her. She was having a seizure.

"Please step back," Otis ordered the crowd. "Give
her some room, please. Thank you."

Vince's heart raced as he watched Taja continue to
jerk, but he knew that she'd be fine.

Someone in the crowded gymnasium asked, "Should
we call the paramedics?"

"No," said Otis. "She'll come out of it."

Sasha appeared at Vince's side. She held him around
the waist and watched as Taja jerked for several minutes. Soon, she stopped jerking and became extremely
still and silence filled the gym. Every eye was on Taja as
if it were a show. Her breathing changed and it appeared
that she'd fallen asleep—a deep sleep. She snored even.
Otis shook her out of it.

"Taja, wake up," he ordered. "Taja!" He called her
name a few more times, and she slowly opened her eyes,
looking disoriented.

She glanced around the room, trying to make sense
of where she was and what had happened.

"There's an office in the back," said Vince. "Let's
take her there."

Otis lifted Taja into his arms and pushed through
the crowd, calling out, "Excuse me…coming through."

He followed Vince to an empty office in the gym. Sasha came along, as well. Otis placed Taja atop the desk and kissed her forehead.

"You okay, baby?" he asked.

"My head hurts," said Taja.

"What happened?" Vince asked, trying to make sense of everything. "Was it because I put her back in the game?"

"It's her meds. She's missed a couple of doses," he explained. "She rarely has seizures, because we keep them under control with her meds. But she ran out and I wasn't able to fill her prescription. Damn it!" he yelled at the top of his lungs.

"Look, bro. You've got to let me help you. There's no way around it. Taja's life is in danger if she doesn't get the proper medication on a consistent basis," Vince said. He was becoming angry over the situation. "I know that you're a man with pride, but everyone needs a little help from time to time. I'm filling her prescription myself, and that's the end of it."

"This is all your fault." Otis pointed his long finger in Sasha's face. "You and your crooked law firm. Did you think I wouldn't find out? Did you think I wouldn't know that you were the attorney assigned to my case? You and your fancy talk, pumping me for information, all the while representing the scumbags who fired me!"

"What?" Vince asked, trying to make sense of things. "What are you talking about, Otis? Sasha, what is he talking about?"

Otis answered first. "She's the lead attorney on the case against me. She represents ProTek. She's defending them."

"Is this true?" Vince asked Sasha.

"Yes, my firm represents ProTek. And yes, I was assigned to the case—"

"Did you know this when we met with Otis in my dental office that day?"

"Not at first. Not until—"

"So you knew and you didn't say anything?" Vince interrupted.

"Yes, but—"

"Yes, but what?" Vince asked.

"Yes, but I wanted to tell you. It was never the right time…"

Otis interrupted. "She pumped me for information that she could use against me in court. And that's just wrong."

"I need some air." Vince held his hands up and walked toward the door. Sasha tried to grab his arm, but he jerked away.

How could the woman he claimed to love do something so low-down?

By the time he cleared his head and came back inside, Sasha was gone. Taja was up walking around but complained of a headache.

"Let's go by the pharmacy and get that prescription filled," Vince told Otis.

"I'm going to pay back every dime I owe you," Otis said.

"You don't owe me anything," Vince said, and he meant every word.

After dropping Otis and Taja off, Vince slowly drove away. The day's events had left him baffled—and possibly without Sasha in his life. He couldn't be with someone who was unethical, or who treated people with blatant disrespect. There was a point in which doing the right thing trumped your career. And if she didn't know that, then she wasn't the type of woman he wanted to spend his life with.

Chapter 21

Sasha was stubborn. As much as she wanted to pick up the phone and call Vince, she couldn't bring herself to do it. And he hadn't bothered to call her either. If he wasn't going to give her the benefit of the doubt, then he certainly wasn't the type of man she wanted to spend her life with. He hadn't given her a chance to explain that she'd removed herself from the case when she found out there was a conflict. She missed him but was glad that he'd shown his true colors early on. He was judgmental, in her opinion. And she was glad to rid her life of him once and for all.

Love wasn't all that complicated, she thought. Once you closed your mind to all possibilities of it, you were well on your way to having an uncomplicated life. That's what she had before Vince waltzed into it. He'd come in and shook things up, changed things around and then disappeared. She wouldn't let anyone do that again.

She would have joined her family at their small church in Fayetteville for a Sunday morning service, but she wasn't in the mood today. Instead she glanced at the television, where her favorite TV evangelist was asking for support of his megaministry.

It had been weeks since Sasha did Sunday dinner at her parents' house. She'd always come up with some excuse: she had a deposition on Monday and needed to prepare, she had a new client or she had a rough week and needed to rest. Usually, she would pop a frozen dinner into the microwave and then curl up on the sofa with a law book or someone's file in hand. That was Sunday dinner.

But today, she'd dressed in a pair of skinny jeans, a nice cardigan and knee-length boots. Her hair was styled to perfection, and her eyes danced with a natural shade of brown on her eyelids. She stopped by the corner bakery, picked up a New York-style cheesecake and then headed to her parents' home in Fayetteville.

Sasha parked her car in the circular drive behind Bridget and Derrick's SUV. When she stepped up to the front door carrying the dessert, she could hear Vanessa's children running around inside. They were laughing, and when she stepped inside the door, all three of them rushed up to her and gave her hugs.

"Hi, Sasha!" the oldest one yelled. "Everyone's in the kitchen."

"Are they?" She picked up the two-year-old and held her in her arms for a moment. "Have you been good?"

The toddler nodded her head yes, and Sasha placed her back onto the floor then kissed the forehead of the middle child.

She could hear her father's and Derrick's banter in the family room. They watched football on the family's big-screen television. There was laughter and loud conversations coming from the kitchen, which is where Sasha headed to first.

"Well, look who's here!" Vanessa spotted Sasha first.

"Hi, Vanessa." Sasha gave her cousin a hug. "Love your hair."

"Well, Mother, if it isn't your long-lost daughter who rarely shows up for Sunday dinners." Bridget gave her a wicked look. "We're glad you could join us."

Sasha approached her mother and kissed her cheek.

"Hi, sweetheart, we're so glad you're here." Charlotte placed her hand gently on Sasha's face. "And you're looking so pretty. What is going on with you? You look different."

"She looks like she's getting some," Bridget stated inappropriately and then winked.

Sasha hadn't shared with her sister that she and Vince had broken up.

"Bridget! Behave," their mother warned.

"I brought dessert," Sasha announced with a grin, totally ignoring her sister.

"Is it store-bought?" Vanessa asked. "Because you know we don't do no store-bought desserts around here. I make the best sweet potato pie this family has ever known."

"That's very conceited," Sasha teased.

"The truth is the truth, honey," Vanessa boasted.

"And her chocolate cake is to die for," Bridget announced.

Sasha placed the cheesecake in the refrigerator and headed for the family room, where her father was. She knew she'd receive a favorable reception from her daddy.

"We missed you at church this morning!" her mother yelled as she left the kitchen.

Sasha didn't respond.

"Who's winning?" she asked as she stepped into the family room.

"Sasha, baby!" The excitement on her father's face was priceless. "Get over here."

Sasha plopped down on the sofa next to her father and he wrapped his arm around her neck and kissed her cheek. She needed that.

"Hey, Derrick," said Sasha.

Derrick wore an Atlanta Falcons jersey and held on to a bottle of beer. "Good to see you, sis."

"It's been a long time since you've come for Sunday dinner. We've missed you," Brian Winters said while holding on to his daughter.

"I know, Daddy. I've just been busy."

"You have to make time for family. When work is gone, all you have left are the people who love you. Please come by more often," Brian said.

"I will. I promise."

"Good."

"How's Vince?" Derrick asked.

She wasn't sure how to respond, so she said, "I haven't talked to him in a few weeks."

"What? I thought you two talked every day."

"Not anymore."

"He didn't say anything," Derrick said. "What happened?"

"Just didn't work out."

"Vince is the guy I played a round of golf with in the Bahamas, right?" her father asked. "The best man at the wedding?"

"Yes, that's him," Derrick answered for her while never taking his eyes off the television screen.

"Were you dating him, honey?"

"Who's she dating?" her mother asked as she approached the room.

"No one," Sasha answered abruptly.

"Derrick's friend, Vince," her father answered for her. "The one we met in the Bahamas."

Suddenly Charlotte remembered. "Oh, yeah, the young man who whipped you in golf."

"He does have a pretty good handicap," Brian stated.

"Is that who you're seeing now?" asked Charlotte. "What does he do for a living?"

"Seeing who?" Bridget asked and then plopped down on the sofa next to her husband. She was eating a huge plateful of chocolate cake.

Derrick took the plate from her hand. "Not good for the baby," he said and gave her a peck on the lips.

Bridget rolled her eyes at her husband, but then smiled. He finished her cake in one bite. Sasha zeroed in on Bridget's stomach. She noticed that there was a small pouch forming in her midsection and she'd gained a few pounds.

"She's seeing Vince." Charlotte had taken a few words of a conversation and formulated a conclusion.

"Duh…yeah! They've been knocking boots for a while now." Bridget giggled.

"Since the Bahamas," Vanessa chimed in.

Her father always had a way of coming to her rescue. "Whether she's seeing him or not, it's none of our business. Sasha's a grown woman." He gave her a wink.

Nobody said a word. She gave her father a warm smile.

Sasha stood and pushed past her mother and Vanessa. "I'm going to fix my plate," she said.

Bridget followed Sasha to the kitchen.

"What's up, Sash? Did you and Vince break up?"

"We weren't really dating officially," Sasha said.

"Well, you were doing something," said Bridget, "and you were happy. So what happened?"

"It's a long story."

"I have all day. Come on, girl! Don't do the same thing you did when you broke up with Kevin. You went into this deep depression, and it felt like you never came out," Bridget said. "We used to be so close and could talk about any and everything."

"I'm fine, Bridget," Sasha claimed.

"Sasha, stop trying to handle everything all by yourself. You were there for me when I needed you most. Let me be there for you."

Sasha sighed. Tears began to fill her eyes. They came out of nowhere. Bridget grabbed her by the hand and took her upstairs to one of the guest bedrooms before anyone could see her crying. She eased the door shut behind them.

"Now, start talking."

"I made a mistake," Sasha began. "Vince's friend was wrongly fired from his company because he refused to engage in unethical behavior. He lost everything—his job, his car…he's almost homeless. He'd already filed a motion against them, but he couldn't afford the attorney he'd hired."

Bridget took it all in.

"Anyway, the guy was broke and needed legal help, so I recommended Robin. Only Robin was in Africa and couldn't take the case…" Sasha was babbling and she was sure she'd lost Bridget somewhere along the way, so she decided to get to the heart of the matter. "Turned out, the company in question was my client."

"Isn't that some type of conflict of interest?"

"Yeah, it is. Which is why I marched right into Kyle's office a few days later and removed myself from the case."

"But Vince was mad because it seemed that you were trying to hurt his friend?"

"And that I withheld information from him."

"Did you explain what happened?"

"He never gave me a chance. He just walked away. Didn't let me explain anything." Sasha wiped tears from her eyes. "I said I wasn't going to cry over him. If he's not willing to give me the benefit of the doubt, then he's not the man I thought he was."

"I feel you on that. Maybe you can just call and talk to him about it."

"I think he should call me…clear the air."

"You're being stubborn, Sasha. There's nothing wrong with giving him a call and explaining your case. Be the bigger person."

"Why should I be the bigger person?"

"Because you're crazy about him," said Bridget. "You were so happy. I wish you could work it out."

"It's over between us, Bridge. I don't even know if I want to work it out."

"Of course you do. It's not the end of the world, Sash."

It felt like it. It seemed as if Sasha's world had ended that day in the gym when Vince walked away. All those familiar feelings of being hurt had rushed right back to the forefront. The hurt of losing Kevin was painfully there, staring her in the face, and she realized that she'd never healed. Instead she'd fought hard to bury her feelings in work—never really coming to terms with the pain and vowing never to feel that way again.

Chapter 22

Vince bumped his head as he climbed down from the attic. He had carefully inspected his mother's furnace and changed all the filters. He had replaced the batteries in her smoke alarms and insulated her attic. It was his annual ritual of preparing her home for the winter. Though Atlanta winters weren't as brutal as those in the northern states, temperatures still dipped low enough to make one bundle up in front of a warm, cozy fire.

He stacked firewood in front of the fireplace while Dolores prepared all his favorite foods. The house smelled of cinnamon and other spices, and an apple pie baked in the oven. It was no surprise she spoiled her grown son. Some might even refer to him as a mama's boy if they didn't take a closer look. A sharper eye would see that he spoiled her, as well. It was his duty to take care of the women in his life.

When Vince was a teenager, he'd taken his role as

man of the house very seriously. It was during those years that he'd truly learned what it meant to be a man. He had a job and responsibilities back then.

"You've been spending an awful lot of time over here lately, Vincent," his mother said as he replaced the last lightbulb in the upstairs hallway. "You seem sad, honey. What's going on?"

"I think I messed up, Ma."

There was no dancing around it. "What have you done?"

"I misjudged someone, and now I don't know how to fix it."

He explained the details of the situation to his mother. Dolores listened intently.

"I found out later that she had removed herself from the case."

"How did you find that out?"

"My friend Otis did some poking around and learned what she'd done. I think I might've forced her hand."

"Or maybe she'd already made her own decision about it," Dolores said. "Why didn't you apologize when you found out?"

"It was too late. Things were too far gone."

"Or was it that you were too embarrassed?" His mother was perceptive.

Vince nodded his head yes.

"It's okay to make mistakes, Vincent. You're not a perfect man. You're simply a man. And part of being a man means admitting when you're wrong and correcting whatever needs to be fixed."

"I'm sure she won't hear anything I have to say at this point."

"How will you know if you don't try?"

"Because she's stubborn and strong-willed."

"Hmm…like someone else I know."

Vince followed his mother to the kitchen, where she cut him a nice hunk of apple pie.

"You think I can make this right with her?" he asked.

"Only you know the answer to that," his mother said. "Do you love her?"

"So much, Ma."

"Then you have to let her know."

As Vince sat at his mother's kitchen table, he knew what he needed to do. He'd been wrong about Sasha, and he'd allowed his pride to get in the way. Experience had taught him that a prideful man was in danger of losing everything. In his opinion, he'd done just that. He'd lost the woman of his dreams. He'd fought so hard to win her heart in the first place. Winning it again might be an even greater challenge. But he was a man who went after the things he wanted—and almost always got them.

Chapter 23

It had been a while since she'd had lunch at the social club with her mother. Sasha hated that place and the uppity people who gathered there. It seemed that everyone was making this great attempt to be something they weren't and trying to impress each other with their material things. Her mother had been a member for years. She'd become quite close with the wives of mayors, aldermen and other political and social figures of the Atlanta community. She'd often encouraged Sasha to rub elbows with them, claiming that making partner at her firm was more about whom she knew and not what she knew.

Sasha was never one to use her affiliations with others to advance her career. She wanted to achieve partner because she was a great attorney, not because her mother knew people in high places.

"I'm glad you could pull yourself away for lunch,"

said Charlotte. "It's been a long time since we've had some girl time—just me and you."

The truth was they'd never had much girl time. Sasha and her mother had nothing in common, and every encounter seemed strained. Sasha felt as if her mother didn't respect her career and had no confidence in her decisions as a woman. Charlotte felt that Sasha pushed her away and didn't give her half the respect that she gave her father.

"We don't really have girl time, Mother. You know that."

"It's not because I don't want to. In fact, I'd like to change that, which is why I invited you here for lunch. When you were a little girl, I took you along with me everywhere I went. You were my little sidekick. I'd dress you up in one of those pretty little dresses..."

"I'm not a little girl anymore. I'm a grown woman."

"I know that, Sasha."

"Then why do you keep treating me like I'm still this little girl who doesn't have a brain of her own? I'm an accomplished attorney, yet you won't even acknowledge my accomplishments."

"I think that you're always so busy, Sasha. Always on the go. And you should settle down, find a man and have some babies."

"Have some babies?"

"Yes, your father and I are looking forward to being grandparents. We were elated to find out that Bridget is having a new little one."

"Really?"

"Yes."

"You were grandparents years ago. Remember?"

"What are you talking about?"

"Remember when Bridget was sixteen? The baby she

was forced to abort because it was too inconvenient for you? Weren't you grandparents then?"

"Sasha, that was a long time ago. And we all agreed that we would never discuss that again."

"No, you agreed!"

"I made the best decision for Bridget. She wasn't capable of raising a child back then. She was too young. Now she's grown and married."

"She was traumatized because of it. And so was I."

"I won't apologize for making the best decision that I could possibly make for my underage daughter."

"What about me? Did you think it was the best decision for me?"

"It didn't have anything to do with you!"

"It did! I was right there witnessing the whole thing. Listening to Bridget cry herself to sleep every night for months…"

Charlotte was quiet for a moment. It was the first she'd heard of Bridget crying over the unborn child.

"You're so strong, Sasha. I don't worry about you."

"I'm not as strong as you think I am, Mother. I needed you, and you were never there for me."

"It's because you push everyone away, Sasha. Everyone who loves you. You bury yourself in your work, and no one knows how to reach you," said Charlotte.

"I'm here. I'm reachable. But you don't reach for me. I embarrass you, because I won't do things the way you think they should be done."

Charlotte was silent and contemplated her daughter's comments.

"I think you make life harder than it has to be, Sasha."

"You don't know me at all," Sasha continued.

"I know you very well. You're my daughter, and

you're just like your father. You're stubborn. I wanted you to be more like me, but you chose to follow in his footsteps."

"I'm not hungry anymore," said Sasha. "I have to get back to work. I have a deposition this afternoon."

Sasha stood and grabbed her purse.

"You're always running away, Sasha. When are you going to learn to face things?"

Sasha walked away from the table and made a bee-line for her car before the tears fell. She drove back to the office in silence. She'd gotten some things off her chest, and that felt good.

Robin looked exhilarated. Africa had done her a world of good. Her skin was perfect and flawless; everything about her was natural and wonderful. Along with the fresh catch of the day, she ordered every sushi roll on the Atlanta Fish Market's menu.

"As you can see, I've missed this place!" Robin exclaimed when she tasted the mahimahi.

"Me too. I haven't been here in quite a long time," Sasha replied. "Too long."

"You have some things on your heart. I can always tell with you, Sasha. You're so transparent. What's going on?"

"I'm ready for a career change."

She'd expected a look of shock from Robin, but she didn't get it. Instead, Robin munched on her spicy tuna roll as if she hadn't eaten in days. She didn't even flinch.

Sasha had made up her mind about it. She had finally grown tired of Johnson, Johnson and Donovan. With Louis retiring, she knew that working with Kyle would be nearly impossible.

"Did you hear me?"

"Of course I did. I knew you would come around once you discovered that you were too bright to continue to work for that firm. You're too good for them," Robin said. "You ready to partner with me?"

"If the offer still stands."

"I'm delighted. When can you start?"

"I would like to give them two weeks' notice. Louis deserves that."

"That's fine."

"I have a small request, though."

"What is it?"

"I have a legal assistant who is phenomenal. I'd like to bring her along."

"She must be good if Sasha Winters is bringing her along. Ironically, I just posted an ad in the classifieds for a new legal assistant," Robin said. "Whatever they're paying her over there, we'll match it. And maybe we can increase it in a few months."

"She knows more about law than half the attorneys on staff."

"Then maybe she should go to law school and take the bar."

"Maybe she should." Sasha's heart warmed at the thought of helping Keira.

"I'm so happy, Sasha! You know this has been a long time coming. You're finally taking a leap of faith, and I'm so proud of you."

"It's like we've come full circle. I remember when we first passed the bar. I took the internship at Johnson, Johnson and Donovan. You took an internship at Forester and Young. You worked there for what…two years before you walked out on them?"

"Eighteen months. Just long enough to figure things

out. And boy, did I think I had everything all figured out."

"I thought you were crazy going out there on your own. I thought that a more established firm made more sense."

"It did make more sense…for you. You're timid about things. You're afraid to spread your wings and fly. But as for me, I knew it was the right thing to do. I knew it would be hard and I'd have to work my behind off for it, but I don't regret one single moment." Robin moved her hair out of her face while dipping her California roll into sauce. "I do a lot of good things for people. And when I go home at night, I feel absolutely great about what I do…the people I help."

"That's what I want, Robin."

"You deserve it, too." Robin held her hand out. "I guess a handshake would be the proper way to seal our new business relationship."

Sasha took her hand in a firm shake. "I guess it would be."

Robin flagged down the server, calling him by name. "Sergio, please bring us the best bottle of champagne you have. We're celebrating!"

"Yes, ma'am," said Sergio. "I'll be right back."

Sergio disappeared, and Sasha smiled at her new business partner. She was anxious to start her new life.

When Sasha returned to her office, she stopped by Keira's desk and picked up a stack of messages. She had two calls from clients and three from Vince.

"He said he's been calling your cell and you won't pick up," Keira explained.

Sasha ignored Keira's comment about Vince and

said, "Come with me to my office. I have something I need to talk to you about."

Keira removed her headset and followed Sasha into her office. Sasha was filled with excitement as she closed the door behind them. She couldn't wait to give Keira the good news. She was taking a leap of faith, and she wanted Keira to jump with her.

She didn't beat around the bush. Time was of the essence because she'd also scheduled a meeting with the partners that would take place in less than five minutes.

"I'm leaving the firm in two weeks. I'll be joining my friend in her private practice. It's a small place, not like the clientele we have here. It's cozy, but the business is consistent. She takes on the clients other attorneys won't give the time of day to. I'd like to take you with me if you'd like to go. It's totally up to you. I don't know what your future plans are, Keira, but you're the best legal assistant in this entire firm. What we're offering is your current salary, with the possibility of an increase in a few months. Now, if you'd like to take some time and think about it…"

"Are you kidding, Sasha?"

"I'm dead serious."

"Thought about it. And yes! I'm going."

"Just like that?"

"Just like that." Keira gave Sasha a hug. "I'm your assistant. So wherever you go, I'm going too! Thank you, Sasha. You've made my day."

"Once we get over there, I'd like to mentor you. You should be a lawyer! I want you to go to law school and take the bar."

"I can't afford law school. And what about the kids?"

"There are scholarships and financial aid. And there

are so many flexible programs for working adults with children. I'm sure you can find one that works for you."

Keira's eyes were moist with tears, and Sasha fought back tears of her own.

"I have to go talk to the partners. Take as much time as you need in here."

"Okay," Keira whispered.

The partners were seated around the conference table—the same conference table that Sasha had sat at a million times discussing cases, formulating plans and being belittled by Kyle Johnson. They all had inquisitive looks on their faces. They wondered what was so urgent that Sasha needed them in the same room at the same time. She took her usual seat next to Louis.

"I won't take up much of your time. I know you're all busy, so I'll make it quick. I will be handing in my official notice of resignation, but I wanted to give you a heads-up first. Two weeks from now I will be leaving the firm to pursue other endeavors. I'd like to thank you, Louis, for giving me a chance as an intern and for believing in me."

"You're quite welcome, Sasha. And you will certainly be missed."

"This is certainly a surprise, Sasha. Is there anything we can do to get you to stay?" asked Matt Donovan.

"No, there isn't. But thank you, Matt. I've enjoyed working with you, and I've learned a lot from you."

"Where are you going?" asked Kyle, who looked defeated.

"I'm going to work with a friend in her private practice," Sasha explained.

"You'll do well, Sasha. You're a brilliant attorney."

Louis smiled and gave her a firm handshake. Matt followed with one also.

"What about this firm and all the cases that you're leaving us with? Don't you care about that?" asked Kyle.

"Well, there's always Kirby. She's certainly a capable attorney. And there are so many bright, young attorneys fresh out of law school who would do well here."

"What about making partner? Don't you care about that anymore?"

"When I leave, I will be someone's partner, Kyle."

"And Louis's corner office with the view?" Kyle seemed to be in the mood for a debate.

"Not so important anymore."

"What changed your mind?" He was certainly inquisitive. "Was it Kirby?"

"There were many factors, Kyle. The least of which was Kirby."

"Well, Sasha, I wish you the best," Kyle finally said, "but keep my number just in case. It's a rat race out there. You might need it."

Sasha didn't bother to respond to his comment. Instead she stood and said, "Well, gentlemen, thank you for your time."

"Sasha, if you don't mind, I'd like a word with you first," said Kyle.

Realizing that he meant he wanted a private word with Sasha, Louis and Matt stood, left the room and closed the conference room door behind them.

Kyle moved inappropriately close to her.

"Why are you really leaving, Sasha? Is it because I've neglected you?" His finger reached for her face, and she grabbed it before it reached its destination. However,

Kyle didn't stop there. He grabbed her by the waist and tried to kiss her. She pushed him away and slapped him.

She left the conference room in a hurry. She felt free. For the first time in a long time, Sasha Winters felt free.

Chapter 24

Thanksgiving had always been a big deal in the Winters family, particularly since November was also the month of Sasha's parents' wedding anniversary. Each year, the family would gather for a dinner party and celebrate the couple's life and love. They'd invite friends and family near and far. Usually the event was catered and would take place at the family's five-bedroom home where Sasha and Bridget grew up. And this year was no different.

The house was decorated in different shades of red with black undertones. Vases filled with red roses adorned every table in the room. Red and black streamers hung from the ceiling. Sasha's uncle Richard played soft music on the grand piano in the living room. Occasionally his wife would join him in a duet, or one of Sasha's cousins would jazz up an old song. Love was definitely in the air.

Sasha usually wore something demure—a simple pantsuit or a modest dress, one that she'd wear to church or to the office. But this year, she looked ravishing in the red midthigh-length cocktail dress, the one that Vince had picked out when they spotted it at Cumberland Mall several weeks before. They'd met at the mall for a matinee at the movie theater—after which they'd popped into every store just to take a look at the merchandise. That was back when he had a presence in her life.

She'd thought of him often over the past few weeks. She missed him—missed his smile. She missed his quirkiness and their long conversations about their past and present lives. She missed how he looked at her with desire and how he made her body feel so alive every time he touched her. She missed his cologne and those valleys he called dimples.

"Do you think this is too sexy?" She had popped out of the dressing room at Macy's.

He'd been speechless for a moment, but had managed to say, "Wow—I think it's absolutely sexy and perfect on you."

"You think so?"

"Did you look at yourself in the mirror before you came out here?" he'd asked.

"Yes." She blushed.

"Obviously you didn't. Come here." He grabbed her and took her to a mirror. "You look absolutely gorgeous."

She and Vince hadn't even defined their relationship. They hadn't even discussed where it was headed. They never got to that point. They were living in the moment, and she had enjoyed every minute of it.

* * *

When Sasha walked through the door at her parents' house, every eye was on her. Besides the sexy dress that she wore, her face was glowing. Her mother was the first to approach her.

"Well, look at you, Sasha Winters. You look…"

"Fabulous," said Bridget, who had quickly approached. "What the heck is going on with you, Sasquatch? You look…"

"Beautiful," said her father, who gave her a hug and a kiss on the cheek. "Baby, you look breathtaking."

Charlotte took Sasha's hand. "Your aunt Myrtle has been asking for you all night. You should go say hello to the old woman."

Aunt Myrtle was Charlotte's older sister and Sasha's favorite aunt. She was Sasha's complete opposite, but someone she'd like to be in her next life. Aunt Myrtle was witty and outspoken. She was the life of the party, with her diva wig to the side and a dress that crept well above her knee. She was always accompanied by a man who was half her age.

"Is that my ladybug?" she asked.

"Hey, Aunt Myrtle." Sasha gave her aunt a hug and made reference to the young man standing a few feet away. "I see that some things never change."

"You know your old auntie is still full of life." Aunt Myrtle winked and held her drink in the air—a vodka with orange juice, her favorite. "And look at you. Who's the new man?"

"What?"

"Oh, honey, it's so obvious. Your face is beaming like the sunshine. And that dress…girl, you are wearing the hell out of that dress. If I was twenty years younger and about thirty pounds lighter, I'd squeeze my big behind into that one. Yes I would." Aunt Myrtle giggled. "So tell me about him."

Aunt Myrtle had always been someone she could talk to and share secrets with.

"He's gorgeous, of course," said Sasha. "Intelligent, mysterious...the perfect gentleman."

"You love him?"

"We're not together anymore."

"It isn't that funny-looking guy your sister brought here tonight, is it?"

"What guy?" Sasha asked.

Before Aunt Myrtle could respond, Bridget popped up out of nowhere.

"And this is my sister, Sasha," she was saying.

When Sasha turned around, she was face-to-face with a short, vanilla-colored man dressed in gray slacks and a simple white dress shirt.

"It's so nice to finally have a conversation with you, Sasha. Your sister has told me so much about you. I'm Paul." He held out his hand.

Sasha took his hand in a firm handshake. *The infamous Paul who drives around town in a Maserati,* she thought.

"Nice to meet you, Paul," Sasha said cordially.

"Bridget tells me you work for a firm in downtown Atlanta."

"Johnson, Johnson and Donovan."

"Yes, I'm familiar with the Johnsons," said Paul. "I play golf with Kyle."

"How nice," Sasha said, and then attempted to walk away. "It was good meeting you, Paul, but I really have a lot of mingling to do."

"You think we can go out sometime, maybe for a bite to eat or a movie?"

When hell freezes over, she wanted to say. But instead she was interrupted by Aunt Myrtle.

"I'm sorry to interrupt whatever you got going on here, son," said Aunt Myrtle, "but I need to steal my niece away for just a moment."

Before Paul could protest, Aunt Myrtle had grabbed Sasha's hand and whisked her away to the opposite side of the house.

"Thank you so much, Aunt Myrtle. I owe you one."

"I figured you needed to be rescued." Aunt Myrtle smiled. "Now, tell that sister of yours to mind her own business and stay out of yours. Why did you break up with your sweetie anyway? Did somebody cheat?"

"No, nothing like that."

"Is he gay?"

"Aunt Myrtle, you're something else." Sasha laughed aloud this time. She loved her aunt.

"So I've been told."

"No, he's not gay. He would've loved you." Sasha smiled.

"Most people don't really know how to take me," Aunt Myrtle said and handed Sasha her glass. "Now, go get me another drink, would you?"

"Yes, ma'am," said Sasha as she crept across the room, making sure to carefully avoid any interaction with Paul again.

She maneuvered to the wet bar, which Derrick stood behind pouring drinks for the guests. He'd been designated as the bartender for the night.

"What's up, Sasha?" He grinned.

"Hey, Derrick. I need a vodka and orange juice."

"Is it that bad? You're drinking vodka and orange juice now?"

"It's for Aunt Myrtle."

Derrick laughed and pulled a shot glass from the shelf. "One vodka and orange juice coming up."

"And I'll have a Black Russian," said the familiar voice behind her. "No, make it a Dirty Black Russian."

Vince leaned with his elbow against the bar and moved in closer to Sasha. He looked dashing in his black suit, and his cologne danced across her nose. His smile was grander than the piano in her parents' living room, and his eyes longed for her. Someone had invited him, and she wasn't sure whom, but she was happy to see him.

Derrick handed the vodka and orange juice to Bridget, who had walked up.

"I'll take this to Aunt Myrtle." She winked at Sasha.

Derrick made Vince a Dirty Black Russian and placed it on the bar.

Vince grabbed the drink, never removing his eyes from Sasha. "Can we go somewhere and talk?"

"I don't know where we would go. There're people in every inch of this house."

"Except the garage," Derrick interrupted. "Nobody's out there."

Sasha gave him a sideways look and rolled her eyes at him. Vince followed Sasha as she led him through the house, through the kitchen and to the garage. Her father's old truck was parked out there. Tools hung along the walls, and a riding mower sat in the corner. Sasha took a seat on her father's workbench.

"You cold?" Vince asked.

Sasha nodded a yes and he removed his jacket and wrapped it around her bare arms.

"I'm sorry, Sasha. I was so wrong. I judged you, and I'm sorry. I didn't give you the benefit of the doubt. I heard what Otis said, but I didn't give you the opportunity to tell your side of the story."

"No, you didn't."

"Can you find it in your heart to forgive me?"

Sasha's heart was racing. She wasn't over Vince as she'd pretended to be.

"It really hurt when you walked away like that and didn't give me a chance to explain."

"All I kept thinking was that I couldn't be with someone who could treat a human being that way, a woman who could think only of her career and not the livelihood of someone in need."

"After my conversation with Otis, I knew that I had to remove myself from the case. That's what I was trying to tell you at the gym…that his facts were wrong. That I wasn't the attorney handling his case anymore. But everybody's emotions were all high…and…"

"And your man was being a fool." He finished her sentence.

"Were you my man?"

"I felt like I was your man. I felt like you were my woman."

"If I was your woman, you should've protected me."

"If you allow me to be your man again, I'll never fail to do that again."

He was wearing her down. Her emotions were in a tizzy.

"Can I have another chance to take care of you, to protect you, Sasha?" Vince caressed her face. "Can I be your man again?"

"I don't know if…"

"I've missed you so much. My life has not been the same without you in it. I need you, Sasha. I love you," he whispered.

Before she could respond, he'd pulled her up from the workbench. His lips touched hers. She didn't fight it. She embraced his kiss. His tongue danced inside her mouth. He wrapped his strong arms around her and held her close. He stayed that way for a long time—until she agreed to give him another chance.

Vince unlocked her front door. He wrapped his arms around her from behind as they went inside. She went directly to her bedroom and Vince followed. She stood at the edge of the bed and Vince began to undress her. He started with her heels. He took them off one by one and tossed them across the room. He slowly unzipped her dress and lifted the spaghetti straps from her shoulders. Very carefully he eased the dress from her body, all the while planting kisses along her neck and shoulders. He unsnapped her strapless bra and removed her panties.

Sasha lay across the bed. Leaning up on her elbows, she watched as he undressed himself. He quickly tossed his jacket onto the chair in the corner and removed his shirt. She helped with his buckle. She liked that part. It gave her a thrill to undo his pants. She loved the anticipation in his eyes when she touched his tender places. He stepped out of his pants and quickly removed his briefs.

"Wait a minute," she whispered. "I forgot something."

She rushed into the living room, sorted through the tattered album covers and found Nina Simone's. She pulled the album out of its cover and placed it on the turntable, and Nina's voice echoed through the house, bouncing from the walls.

When she returned to the bedroom, Vince lay flat

on the bed. He reached for her and she climbed on top of him. Her lips found his. He kissed her breasts with a beautiful gentleness before pulling her down onto him. They moved in a certain rhythm—one that only the two of them knew. It was as if their bodies had a language of their own, and they were the only two who understood it. He flipped her over onto her back, slid between her legs and pushed his way into her body again.

After the lovemaking ended, Vince collapsed onto the bed next to Sasha. He held her in his arms tightly, their legs intertwined.

"I quit my job this week," she said softly.

"You did what?" Vince leaned up over her and looked at her with amazement.

"I gave the firm my two-week notice."

"Really?"

"I'm going into private practice with a good friend of mine," she explained. "I realized that I wasn't happy at Johnson, Johnson and Donovan. That I wasn't the least bit fulfilled. I want to be in a place where I can help people like Otis to fight the big companies that prey on the average man."

"He wants to talk to you, by the way. Wanted to apologize for everything that went on."

"He doesn't owe me an apology. I commend him for fighting back. Perhaps he'll let me represent him once I leave the firm."

"You would do that?"

"I would be honored," Sasha said. "I'd get him a nice settlement."

"He found another job. And a car, too. He and Taja are doing well."

"I'm glad."

"I'm so happy at this moment, Sasha. You don't know how lost I was without you."

"Did I hear you say the *L* word in my parents' garage?"

"What, that I love you?"

"Yes."

"That's exactly what I said…I love you, Sasha Winters."

"I love you too."

With that, Sasha fell asleep in his arms. All was well in her world.

When the sunlight crept across her face the next morning, she opened her eyes and looked at Vince. He slept peacefully in her bed, and her life felt complete. In her parents' garage he'd asked to be her man, and her heart danced. It was what she'd wanted—to define their relationship. Put a label on it. She was his woman, and he was her man. And that was all that mattered.

Epilogue

Donny Hathaway's "This Christmas" played loudly through the room. It was a song that always got Sasha in the mood for Christmas. It was her favorite Christmas song ever. She hung up with her client and stepped out of her office then planted her behind on the edge of Keira's desk. Robin danced through the office carrying a bottle of champagne and three glasses. She handed Keira one and Sasha one, and then carefully poured champagne into each of their glasses.

"Here's to a dynamic threesome!" Robin cheered.

"Here, here!" said Sasha. "And to Keira enrolling in law school today."

"Here, here!" Robin held her glass into the air.

With a clang of the glasses, the women sipped.

Vince, wearing a tuque, poked his head inside the door.

"Hi," he said with huge sexy grin—one that made Sasha's heart soar. "I have a surprise for you ladies."

They waited with anticipation as he rushed to his truck and then appeared several minutes later.

"You ready?" he asked before coming in from the cold.

"Yes!" they said in unison.

He opened the door wider and pushed his way inside, carrying a huge Christmas tree. "Merry Christmas!" he exclaimed.

"Oh, wow, babe!" said Sasha.

"How pretty!" Robin exclaimed. "Put it right over here, in front of this window."

Vince lifted the tree, careful not to scratch the hardwood floors. He placed the tree in front of the office's picture window and steadied it on its stand.

"The evergreen smells so good." Keira stood and walked around to the front of her desk.

"Baby, that is a beautiful tree." Sasha gave Vince a hug.

Beneath his wool coat, he wore a tan cardigan that accented the brown in his eyes. His boot-cut jeans fit well with his brown Timberland boots. She didn't even mind the stubble on his face. It made him appear bit rugged.

"I have decorations in the storage closet," Robin announced. "Vince, can you give me a hand with them?"

Vince followed Robin to the storage closet and came back carrying a cardboard box filled with ornaments, bulbs and holly.

Keira began singing. "Hang all the mistletoe. I'm going to get to know you better..."

"This Christmas!" Robin joined in.

Sasha sang, "And as we trim the tree, how much fun it's gonna be together..."

"This Christmas!" Robin and Keira sang the chorus.

* * *

Vince stood back and watched the ladies as they decorated the tree and sang Donny Hathaway's song off-key. He poured himself a glass of champagne. As Sasha went around the tree with a stream of lights, she caught Vince's eye. He smiled and blew her a kiss. He was everything she wanted for Christmas and then some. She felt like the luckiest woman in the world.

He held a piece of evergreen in the air and swung it from side to side. "Look what I found."

"Oh, girl, he's got some mistletoe!" Keira took a sip of her champagne.

Sasha dropped the lights and headed toward Vince. She wrapped her arms tightly around his waist. Holding the mistletoe in the air, he kissed her lips with a certain tenderness that she'd become accustomed to. The two of them watched as Robin and Keira put the finishing touches on the tree. When they were done, Vince placed the star on top. Sasha glanced out the window and thought she saw snow flurries bouncing against the glass. It never snowed much in Atlanta—just a few flurries here or there. She went over to the window to get a closer look. The ground was covered with a beautiful white layer.

"It's snowing," she announced.

"Really?" Robin rushed over to the window.

"It's so pretty out there," said Keira, who had joined them.

Vince pulled Sasha to the side.

"I almost forgot," he said and handed her an envelope. "This came in the mail today."

She looked at the postmark. It was something from Nassau, Bahamas—a letter from Clara. She opened the envelope and read it:

Dearest Vince and Sasha:
Greetings in this holiday season. I have enclosed the recipe for the peas and rice that I promised you. I hope that you will enjoy every delectable bite of it. I've come bearing happy news. My Roger is much better and he and I renewed our vows. I love him dearly. I'm so thankful for the time that we have had together—the many years that we have been blessed to spend together. I know that the two of you will be blessed with many years too. It is hard work, but you have to be strong. I wish the two of you many happy years together. If you haven't eloped already, please send me an invitation to the wedding. I promise to be there with bells on. Have a wonderful Christmas, and a spectacular new year!
Clara

Sasha held the letter close to her heart. "That was so sweet!"

As Vince held her in his arms, she couldn't even remember what her life was like before now. She loved her new job. She didn't have an office with a view of downtown Atlanta, but she had a view nonetheless. When she went home at night, she left work exactly where it needed to be left—in the office. A posh office and nice salary were no longer at the top of her must-have list. Happiness was a priority, and she had that.

Sasha walked over to the window near the tree. She breathed on the cold window until it steamed up. In the steam, she drew the picture of a heart with her fingertip. It was her heart that Vince had stolen. So far, he'd taken good care of it, and she prayed that he would continue to treat it with delicacy. He was the man of her dreams. The one she'd waited her whole life for.

He was her man, and she was his woman.

* * * * *

Two classic Eaton novels in one special volume...

FOREVER
AN EATON

NATIONAL BESTSELLING AUTHOR
ROCHELLE ALERS

In *Bittersweet Love*, a tragedy brings history teacher Belinda Eaton and attorney Griffin Rice closer when they must share custody of their twin goddaughters. Can their partnership turn into a loving relationship that is powerful enough to last?

In *Sweet Deception*, law professor Myles Eaton has struggled for ten years to forget the woman he swore he'd love forever—Zabrina Cooper. And just when Myles is sure he's over her, Zabrina arrives back in town. As secrets are revealed, can they recapture their incredible, soul-deep chemistry?

"Smoking-hot love scenes, a fascinating story and extremely likable characters combine in a thrilling book that's hard to put down." —RT Book Reviews on SWEET DREAMS

Available May 2013 wherever books are sold!

www.Harlequin.com

KPRA1260513

REQUEST YOUR FREE BOOKS!

2 FREE NOVELS PLUS 2 FREE GIFTS!

KIMANI™ ROMANCE

Love's ultimate destination!

YES! Please send me 2 FREE Harlequin® Kimani™ Romance novels and my 2 FREE gifts (gifts are worth about $10). After receiving them, if I don't wish to receive any more books, I can return the shipping statement marked "cancel." If I don't cancel, I will receive 4 brand-new novels every month and be billed just $5.19 per book in the U.S. or $5.74 per book in Canada. That's a savings of at least 20% off the cover price. It's quite a bargain! Shipping and handling is just 50¢ per book in the U.S. and 75¢ per book in Canada.* I understand that accepting the 2 free books and gifts places me under no obligation to buy anything. I can always return a shipment and cancel at any time. Even if I never buy another book, the two free books and gifts are mine to keep forever.

168/368 XDN F4XC

Name	(PLEASE PRINT)
Address	Apt. #
City	State/Prov.	Zip/Postal Code

Signature (if under 18, a parent or guardian must sign)

Mail to the **Harlequin® Reader Service:**
IN U.S.A.: P.O. Box 1867, Buffalo, NY 14240-1867
IN CANADA: P.O. Box 609, Fort Erie, Ontario L2A 5X3

Want to try two free books from another line?
Call 1-800-873-8635 or visit www.ReaderService.com.

* Terms and prices subject to change without notice. Prices do not include applicable taxes. Sales tax applicable in N.Y. Canadian residents will be charged applicable taxes. Offer not valid in Quebec. This offer is limited to one order per household. Not valid for current subscribers to Harlequin® Kimani™ Romance books. All orders subject to credit approval. Credit or debit balances in a customer's account(s) may be offset by any other outstanding balance owed by or to the customer. Please allow 4 to 6 weeks for delivery. Offer available while quantities last.

Your Privacy—The Harlequin® Reader Service is committed to protecting your privacy. Our Privacy Policy is available online at www.ReaderService.com or upon request from the Harlequin Reader Service.

We make a portion of our mailing list available to reputable third parties that offer products we believe may interest you. If you prefer that we not exchange your name with third parties, or if you wish to clarify or modify your communication preferences, please visit us at www.ReaderService.com/consumerchoice or write to us at Harlequin Reader Service Preference Service, P.O. Box 9062, Buffalo, NY 14269. Include your complete name and address.

KROM13R

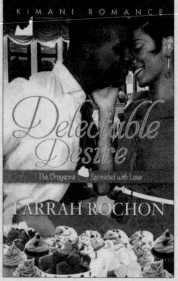